"They thou

findi

"Let them. It will keep them from all manner of foolishness on the trail." Lily glanced at her hand, still captured by his, and then at her skillet. "The turnovers will burn."

Jack didn't care. He wanted to pull her into his lap, bend her over his arm and kiss those red lips.

"Jack. Let go."

He did, and she went about as if nothing had happened. But her cheeks flushed and her nostrils flared as they had when they had climbed that final slope. So, the brief encounter rattled her, as well. It was both disquieting and satisfying to know that he was not alone in his desire.

* * *

Gold Rush Groom

Harlequin® Historical #1055—September 2011

Praise for
Jenna Kernan

OUTLAW BRIDE

"Kernan creates an engaging and fascinating story."
—*RT Book Reviews*

HIGH PLAINS BRIDE

"Those who enjoy Westerns or tales of lovers reunited will not want to miss this book. It has found a place on my keeper shelf and I know I will be reading it again."
—*All About Romance*

TURNER'S WOMAN

"Makes for tip-top reading."
—*RT Book Reviews*

WINTER WOMAN

"Presents a fascinating portrait of the early days of the West and the extraordinary men and women who traveled and settled in the area…Kernan has a knack for writing a solid Western with likable characters."
—*RT Book Reviews*

"WINTER WOMAN is an exciting, no holds barred story with unforgettable characters. Ms. Kernan's first novel is a winner!"
—*Rendezvous*

"With this strong debut, Jenna Kernan puts her name on the list of writers to watch for and WINTER WOMAN may just be the start of a long career."
—*The Romance Reader*

JENNA
GOLD RUSH GROOM
KERNAN

TORONTO NEW YORK LONDON
AMSTERDAM PARIS SYDNEY HAMBURG
STOCKHOLM ATHENS TOKYO MILAN MADRID
PRAGUE WARSAW BUDAPEST AUCKLAND

Recycling programs
for this product may
not exist in your area.

ISBN-13: 978-0-373-29655-2

GOLD RUSH GROOM

This edition published by arrangement with Harlequin Books S.A.

For questions and comments about the quality of this book please contact us at Customer_eCare@Harlequin.ca.

www.Harlequin.com

Printed in U.S.A.

Dedication

With love and gratitude to my prospecting partner
and husband who understands that
what matters is not the treasure, but the hunt.

Available from Harlequin® Historical and
JENNA KERNAN

Winter Woman #671
Turner's Woman #746
The Trapper #768
Wed Under Western Skies #799
"His Brother's Bride"
High Plains Bride #847
Outlaw Bride #883
A Western Winter Wonderland #867
"Fallen Angel"
Sierra Bride #956
His Dakota Captive #1007
Western Winter Wedding Bells #1011
"The Sheriff's Housekeeper Bride"
Gold Rush Groom #1055

Available from Harlequin Nocturne

Dream Stalker #78
Ghost Stalker #111

Author Note

I'm so excited to bring you a story set during the Yukon gold rush. Some of you know that gold prospecting is a hobby of mine and I've hunted from North Carolina to Alaska. I've learned how alluring and elusive gold can be and that surprising things often happen when out on an adventure. In my case that has included keeping a watchful eye out for copperheads while dredging in a North Carolina river and being startled by a bull moose while prospecting in the Brooks Mountain Range.

In this story, Jack Snow, a greenhorn prospector, discovers too late that his steamer ticket does not include transport of his goods from the waterline to the shore. This one unforeseen circumstance nearly costs him everything. He is rescued from disaster by Lily Shanahan, a singer determined to find a partner to get her to Dawson City.

I hope you fall in love with Lily and Jack as you share their dangerous journey.

For more about Jack and Lily please visit me on the web and check out my Story Behind the Story section at www.jennakernan.com.

And, as always, enjoy the adventure!

Chapter One

Dyea, Alaska, Fall 1897

Who among them might be willing to accept an unconventional arrangement? From her vantage point on the muddy beach, Lily Shanahan eyed the newly arrived greenhorns, fresh from the steamer just arrived from Seattle. She knew the wrong choice would mean the end for her, for God only knew the journey to Dawson was perilous, especially now that the freeze-up had begun.

The ship had set anchor far out in the Taiya Inlet to avoid the bore tide that now rushed down the narrow passage. Trapped between the mountains, the water surged forward in long curling waves, hurling the overloaded scows toward the mudflats. The men clung to the gunwales, their faces grim and their eyes wide.

She had seen many arrive this way and depart for the goldfields soon afterward, while she had remained anchored like a rock in a stream. Lily had stopped asking the best candidates. They were not stupid or desperate enough to take her. That left only the ones with obvious flaws. So far they had turned her down as well.

Lily heard her mother's voice as clearly as she had on that final day her mother died. *Sell it all, right down to the sheets I'm lying on and have yourself a life worth remembering.*

And what could be more memorable than joining the mad pulsing rush of stampeders pouring north on the way to the goldfields? But somehow she didn't think her mother had intended her to be marooned by circumstance in these stinking mudflats.

How could she have known, when she spent her last dollar for her ticket, that Dawson City was five hundred miles inland, over mountains and down rivers, a place so wild there were no roads or trains, not even a telegraph? How could she have guessed that it was a journey she could not make alone?

So her search for a partner began. But after nearly a month in this swamp, hauling freight from the muddy beach to the tent town with her dog cart, she'd made a tidy bankroll and had been turned down more times than she could count. Lily longed to be in Dawson by the spring break-up. It was October now, and already the winds blew colder than January in

San Francisco. Would she even see Dawson by next summer?

The first boat scraped up on the mud, beaching as the wave dissipated. The next one rolled in ten feet behind. She knew what would happen next. The poor men would lose everything to the greedy water, while the rich ones would buy protection, paying whatever the haulers demanded to move their precious goods to high ground.

Lily chose potential customers with care, seeking a possible match. Her huge Newfoundland mix, Nala, and her small cart could not handle the larger loads.

Most of the men climbed over the sides into knee-high surf, sucking in their breaths or swearing as the icy water bit through their clothing. The first had just reached the wet mud when the crew began tossing their belongings out like so much rubbish.

One man clutched a single valise, his eyes wide with terror. A wave caught the boat as he tried to jump and fell into the sea. Lily held her breath as he disappeared beneath the crashing water. The oarsman used the paddle to nudge the submerged man toward shore. He came up sputtering and lost his grip on the bag. The tide cast it far past him and then dragged it back before he could wipe the stinging seawater from his eyes. The next wave knocked him down again, but brought his case close to her. Lily lifted her skirts and plucked the soggy suitcase from the surf, hauling it out of harm's way. Nala whined, unhappy when her mistress ventured too close to the sea.

"It's all right, girl." She righted the case and stooped to pat her dog. "Maybe this one will take me."

The man crawled up on the mudflats, spitting up seawater. She had to admit he was a scrawny fellow, but beggars could not be choosers. She felt winter's fast approach like a killing frost. She must get through the pass before the real cold came.

She waited for the man to straighten. He looked even more poorly prepared for Dyea than she had been. He reached for his bag.

"Thanks, missus. You sure saved me."

"You need a cart?" she asked.

"No, missus. I only got this here." He clutched the handle, showing her the suitcase she'd rescued.

"How about a partner?"

"You know a man looking?"

"*I'm* looking."

The little pipsqueak actually had the audacity to laugh.

"Oh, now, I might just as well tie an anvil round my neck as try and haul a woman to Dawson."

She scowled, until she noticed him shivering.

"Camp's that way." She thumbed over her shoulder toward the dunes, beyond which a tent city grew in the mud like mushrooms on a rotting log.

Lily gathered her flagging confidence.

"Come on, Nala."

She picked up several fares and collected her fees. Her purse had never been so large. But her adventure lay over the passes. *A life worth living,* her mother had said, but what had she meant? Lily wasn't sure; death had taken her before she could ask.

Lily lifted her collar against the cold wind that blew off the water. If she made it to Dawson City, would she have enough stories to fill her up like a pitcher of milk, with warm memories and satisfaction?

Stories to tell her children and grandchildren. Lily smiled.

Did you know your old granny once climbed the Chilkoot Pass?

"Did you know she failed and had to go home with her tail between her legs?" Lily pressed her lips together and shook her head. No, she wouldn't.

She lifted her chin and scanned the passengers in the next dinghy hoping, praying for a chance to do as she had promised.

The boat grounded and newcomers scrambled overboard trying vainly to avoid a soaking in icy water. Most had little in the way of property and scampered up the beach like crabs—all except one man. He remained in the punishing surf accepting box after box from the oarsman and tossing them, one after another, the eight-foot distance to the shore.

The undertow should have taken him off his feet, but somehow he held his position.

Lily measured him with her gaze. His clothing looked new and expensive. She judged him to be one of the idle rich who came north out of boredom, unlike those who were driven here by desperate circumstances. He had more gear than any other passenger on the beach. A rich fool, then, with no notion of what to pack and what to leave. Probably had his bloody silver tea service in one of those crates. She hated him on sight, for hadn't she worked sixteen-hour days for men just like this one? But no more. Now she answered only to herself. Her mother would like that.

She expected Pete to cut in front of her, offering his mule team to haul the dandy's gear, but he was far down the beach attending the three launches that had arrived just before this one.

The dandy was all hers. Anticipation coiled in her belly, as she fixed her eyes on the dark-haired man like a hungry rat eyeing an apple core.

She stepped closer. He certainly was big, with none of the flab she associated with men who could afford to eat regularly. She glanced at his hands, noting their size and substance. His shoulders were more than just wide; they seemed to be hung with some quantity of useful muscle. Did he get them boxing in some men's club?

He had secured the load on shore, but now the

next waves shot over his boots to lap at the mountain of cargo, lifting two large crates and dragging them back into the water. He caught both and easily hauled them back to safety. She noted the bulging muscles beneath his fancy new coat as well as the power and agility with which he moved. She estimated the distance of the high-tide line and the speed of the current.

He'd never save it all—not alone anyway. What was in those boxes? Would he do anything to save them?

He looked strong enough, but stamina was needed as well and a drive born from the fear that rich men lacked. A man foolish enough to come here with this many boxes might be foolish enough to accept her offer.

She took a definitive step toward him and then pulled herself up short. What if he turned her down, too? Her cheeks burned with humiliation at the thought. It was one thing to be cast off by one of her own, quite another to be sent packing by this greenhorn dandy. She liked the term greenhorn, once someone had explained that it meant an inexperienced newcomer and compared the men to young animals with new, or green, horns.

He had not noticed her yet, intent as he was at singlehandedly bringing his belongings to high ground. He continued his frantic dance for many minutes, finally coming to complete stillness as he stared out at the inlet. He'd seen it now, the second wave of water reaching ten feet as it rushed toward him. His chin nearly touched his chest. Ah, now that was an expression she recognized—for hadn't she seen that look in the faces of so many hopeless men and women when the jobs dried up back there?

It was a rare thing to witness one of his class brought so low. She savored the moment.

He glanced up. Their eyes met and held. He recognized the truth now; that even he couldn't save it all. She would offer her services and see just what sort of a man fate had cast in her path. It wasn't the offer she wanted to make, but best to test the waters first. She stooped to pat Nala, who sat with her long pink tongue lolling.

Part of her hoped he would turn her down. But surely he couldn't tell by looking at her what she was or where she had come from. She wore fine clothing now and had paid good money for lessons to help eliminate the traces of her Irish heritage that had clung to her every word like cold porridge to a bowl.

Could he?

She set her jaw, gathering her courage. Her desperation eased the next step.

"Would you like help moving your belongings?" She had concentrated hard not to drop the *h* in help.

"*You're* a hauler?"

His clipped New England accent held no hint of the gentle brogue of the Irish. He managed his *h* effortlessly, while simultaneously adding a definite inflection of skepticism. She inclined her head, dignified as a queen.

She took in his black hair and a straight nose that spoke of a childhood which did not include being clouted in the face.

Lily fingered the bump at the bridge of her own nose then dropped her hand, suddenly very self-conscious. All the Shanahans were fighters. No shame in that.

She met his gaze, inhaling sharply at his soulful whiskey colored eyes. He wore no hat and his unruly hair brushed his wide brow. His skin glowed from the exertion with perfect good health. Why he was young, she realized, perhaps only twenty, the same age as Lily. Had his size made her think he was older? He held her gaze and for some reason she couldn't seem to breathe as he looked at her. Her gaze fixed on the curve of his upper lip, the twin lines upon his cheeks that flanked his mouth, the dark stubble that he'd likely scraped away before leaving the steamship this morning. His jaw was wide and the muscles looked strong as if he spent a good deal of his time clenching his teeth.

When she met his eyes again, she felt off-balance and slightly dizzy, as if she were the one who had been dashing in and out of the shifting waves.

The man was handsome as sin, but Lily forced herself to breathe, if a bit more quickly than customarily, for she'd not be caught gawking at him like a child at a candy store window.

"How much?" he asked.

This time she noticed that the rich timbre of his deep voice seemed to vibrate through her insides. She pressed a hand to her middle to gather her flagging resolve.

"I'm not interested in your money."

He frowned. Was he so used to buying everything he needed? She pushed back her indignation. No time for that now.

He quirked a brow, finally fixing her with those arresting eyes before taking the bait. "What would you have from me then?"

"I find myself in need of a partner to Dawson."

His jaw dropped and then he recovered himself and grinned.

"You're joking." He cocked his head. "Are you serious?"

"Deadly."

"Well, I rather think you would be a liability."

She didn't argue, but only glared at him as another three-foot wave beat against his legs, rocking his foundation.

"Well, you're a dark horse yourself, but I'm in a gambling mood."

His eyes widened at the insult. "You think *I'm* a liability? How so?"

How so? She wanted to smack the smug arrogance off his handsome face.

"A greenhorn dandy, with not enough sense to secure his own supplies. Did you think that servants lined the rivers here with the nuggets?"

He lifted his hands to stop her as another wave hit. Two crates smashed together, spilling wood shavings onto the mud.

"Not to worry," she called, "with luck that bore tide will drag you right back to Seattle."

That seemed to strike a nerve, for his face reddened.

A vicious wave crashed into his goods, washing away his indignation. He scrambled to keep hold of his possessions. The ten-foot tidal wave had made half the distance to the shore, rolling a hundred yards beyond the steamer. Lily hoped they had placed the vessel on a long line. She'd seen similar tides take down ships even larger than this one.

"Come, Nala." She placed a hand on her dog's harness and her hound rose.

"A trade," he offered, his voice tinged with desperation. "I have goods."

She turned away.

Damn him and his ten-dollar words. *Liability, my ass.* Doubtful he'd keep his word anyway. Few ever did. Lily gripped Nala's harness and started off. She had wasted enough time.

"Wait!"

She didn't, making him run after her.

He blocked her path, wet to the waist and panting with the exertion of keeping what was more than any one man had a right to hold.

"Be reasonable," he begged.

She laughed, making no attempt to hold down her brogue. "To hell with dat!"

Another wave hit, cresting her boots. It swept away one of his boxes, taking it too far for him to recover, but he tried, rushing into the surf to his knees, preparing to dive and then thought better of it. That showed some sense. Water this cold could cramp the muscles of even the strongest swimmer. She bet he could swim. Probably had private lessons in a pool in Newport. She had learned when her brother had thrown her off a pier one hot July afternoon.

She watched his shoulders droop.

"You need dat?" she called.

He glanced back. His entire face had changed. He looked like a man standing beside an open grave.

"I can't succeed without it."

"If you take me to Dawson, I'll get it fer ye."

He glanced at the box, already twenty yards out and drifting fast. He shook his head in bewilderment. "Yes. I will."

"*All* the way to Dawson?" she clarified.

"Yes!"

With speed born of practice, Lily released Nala's harness and pointed at the box. "Fetch, girl."

Nala barked excitedly and charged into the surf. The dog's webbed feet helped her swim and her thick oily coat seemed impervious to the icy water. Lily stood beside the man, watching her hound cut through the breakers like a black swan, reaching the crate and gripping the edge in her powerful jaws. Nala had it now and Lily knew she'd not let go. In only a few moments the dog had the box ashore and was dragging it over rock and mud with the determination of a St. Bernard making a rescue.

He turned to her, his smile bright with excitement and relief, pinning her with his whiskey eyes. She felt her stomach flutter for the second time. Sand clung to the wet fabric of his new clothing making it look dirty and worn. She took in his disheveled hair and wide flaring nostrils, and realized what was happening between them. Lily tamped down her rising desire. She'd sooner drink seawater than fall for a charmer.

So why did the hair on her neck rise up?

Nala barked excitedly, breaking their trance. The Newfoundland cross frolicked beside the rescued crate, justifiably proud of her accomplishment.

Lily's eyes narrowed on the man. "We have a deal?"

He nodded.

"And in return, I'll look out for you all I can, even after we hit Dawson."

He smiled indulgently, as if he thought a woman could be of little assistance, but offered his hand. She eyed it with suspicion. It was big and broad, the kind that could break a woman's jaw with a moment's carelessness. She pressed her lips together and extended her hand. Long fingers wrapped about hers, cold as seaweed, yet still her stomach fluttered as if just awakening from a long sleep. Lily stepped back from the threat she recognized too late. He felt it, too; she knew it from the new speculation now glittering in his startling eyes.

Suddenly her decision to cast her lot with this stranger seemed more dangerous than the trip to Dawson, because the menace he posed was far more immediate. She knew a man like this could cost her everything. Well, she'd not allow it. She drew herself up, resisting the pull between them as she moved to stand beside her dog even as she eyed him. This was the one she feared would come, the one her mother had warned her about, and she'd just convinced him to spend six months with her as his partner.

Chapter Two

Jack Snow rested one hand on the final crate and stared out at the water that had almost claimed his only chance. They had saved the lot. Together, and with her horse of a hound, they'd reached safety with all his equipment and tools intact. He had read about the tidal bores, of course, but that couldn't compare to riding the mountainous waves that heaved through the narrow inlet. He'd never imagined having to fight one. Now that he and all his goods were past the high-water mark, he stared a moment, finding the phenomenon fascinating. His father would love to see this!

That thought dashed Jack's exaltation as memories rolled in, relentless as any rising tide. There was no sense in looking back. If he was to be his own man, his future lay ahead.

The big dog whined, anxious to get under way. Jack glanced at the beast, happy for the distraction.

The black bitch was strong as any mule, she could swim better than a Labrador and in water as cold as an ice bath. He eyed the huge shaggy creature. How much weight could one dog pull?

The dog's mistress stepped beside her, grounding Jack's thoughts firmly in the here and now. Their eyes met.

Damn it to hell.

The permanence of their arrangement crept over him slowly like a thin layer of ice on a mill pond. He felt sick to his stomach as he thought of all the things that might happen to her while she was in his keeping. Another female in his care, the idea pressed down upon his shoulders, making it hard to breathe. But if he hadn't agreed, then what would become of the two he'd left behind? His carefully laid plans had already begun to crumble like old masonry. He thought he might be sick.

To provide for the two at home, he had to save his gear, and that meant there really was no choice at all. The little hellion had entrapped him as neatly as any spider. With luck, she'd find someone better and drop him like yesterday's news, just like his fiancée had done when she'd heard of his family's ruin.

Why hadn't the available information about the Yukon included something about this mayhem arrival? Jack had planned and studied, taking into account the cold, snow and ice, anticipated river travel and mountain-climbing. He had calculated his supplies and equipment with the excruciating exactitude of the mechanical engineer he had nearly become, taking in every eventuality but one. He had not, in his wildest dreams, imagined that the Pacific Coast Steamship Company would not have constructed a proper dock in Dyea on which to moor their vessel.

Sunk by unforeseen circumstances. Was he no wiser than his father, risking all on one wild venture?

Perhaps not, but he was stronger than his sire, for he'd not cut and run at the first sign of adversity. He might look the part of a dandy, as his new partner had assumed, but he was that man no longer. Circumstances had changed him. Now he needed to succeed just as badly as anyone here. More, in fact. Jack needed to seize the glimmering opportunity to restore what his father had lost—their good name, the respect of his peers, the ability to care for what was left of his family and the future that he still craved. He would reach that gold-bearing gravel in Eldorado Creek so he could try his invention, even if he had to carry this female all the way to Forty Mile.

He glanced at the woman—his partner—giving her a critical once-over. The lift of her pointed chin, the slight curve fixed upon her lips and the narrowing of her eyes made her look both beautiful and wary. No doubt she was trying to size him up as well. He knew she was surprisingly strong for one stricken with such a diminutive body, but she was still only a woman and so his physical and mental inferior. She stood motionless in her crimson coat. Her cuffs and hood were adorned with lush dark fur, possibly wolf. The tight fit showed her to be petite, curvaceous and trim, exactly the type of woman he'd like to bed, but not at all the kind he would choose as a traveling companion. The only thing about her that did not speak of feminine grace was the large Colt repeater strapped to her hip. It seemed impossibly large against her small frame as evidenced by the extra bore holes that kept the wide belt from sliding off her flaring hips. She wore it cinched at the narrowest part of her waist, entirely too high for a quick draw. He wondered if the ancient weapon even fired.

Jack raked both hands through his hair, stopping to cradle his head for a moment as he searched the beach for help. When his gaze finally returned it was to find her studying him.

The woman arrested him with her stunning blue eyes, framed by spiky dark lashes and raven brows that arched as she stared at him in silence. His arms dropped to his sides.

What was she doing here in the first place? Didn't she have family or friends to shelter her? A strong wind might blow her off the mountain.

Surely he could make her see reason. He knew

females had a knack for self-preservation and a proclivity to latch on to the best provider, at least that's what Nancy had done, returning his ring and taking up with Jonathan Martin as quickly after his father's death as propriety permitted. He was a good choice, all in all, with his family's mills lining the Connecticut River from Hartford to Springfield. Was this one like her? If so, he need only find her a better partner to be rid of her.

She leaned forward and he was unable to prevent himself from doing the same. She drew him to her as surely as a magnet draws iron and he could not resist her allure. Her voice was sultry and low, as her breath brushed his cheek like a summer breeze off the Narragansett Bay.

"Don't even think about reneging on our agreement."

He straightened, affronted by her accusation, until he realized he had been thinking that exactly. He'd made an agreement, given his word and yet here he was trying to wiggle out of the deal. He knew what his father would have done in similar circumstances and that made the choice easy.

He met the accusation in her gaze.

"I won't. I'm yours until Dawson."

She laughed. "That's fine then."

What could the little minx possibly think to do inland? She couldn't hope to be a miner—could she?

The work alone would kill her before the ice even froze to the river bottoms.

"What is there in Dawson for you?" he asked, considering that she might be more than she appeared, for here she was alone on a beach making her way without help. If the circumstances were reversed, could he have done as well? He gave her a grudging respect for her pluck.

"Adventure and gold, of course."

Why was he not surprised that she was after riches?

He narrowed his eyes on her, wondering what kind of a woman he had partnered with.

"Adventure?"

She nodded.

"But what will you do there?"

"I can sew or cook or sing. I've done all those and more to make my way here."

"A singer?"

Could he possibly have found a woman who would be more useless on the trail?

"Aren't you the sharp tack? Bet you graduated first in your class."

He hadn't graduated, though he'd been in line to be valedictorian. Likely be Francis Cobbler now. *No, don't think about those days, back when you had everything ahead of you, before the world crumbled beneath your feet.*

If she noticed his sour mood turning icy cold, she

gave no sign, merely laughed, a musical tinkling sound that made the muscles of his abdomen tighten.

"Gold is quite difficult to extract."

Her smile turned his insides to oatmeal. "Oh, there's more to life than gold. And anyway, I'll not starve." She placed a hand on her hip and smiled coquettishly. "And I've a life to live, if I can get over those fool mountains." She gave him a direct stare, reminding him without a word of the promise he had made. He'd never met a woman like her. And what was she talking about, life being more than gold? Obviously, but most of those here were not arriving for the fun of freezing in the passes. He could not figure her.

She gave him a questioning look, her sculpted brows lifting. "We will make it, won't we?"

He couldn't think when he looked at her. Why was he thinking about kissing her? Perhaps it was the nearly irresistible temptation of her raspberry-colored lips.

As the woman waited for some response, she rested her hand easily on the grip of her pistol as if it were a walking stick. Did she not expect him to uphold his end of the bargain? Well, he would.

He couldn't keep the growl from rumbling in his throat. "We'll make it."

That made her smile.

"Yes, we will." She stroked the black dog's head. The beast closed its eyes to savor her mistress's touch and Jack found himself suddenly and unreasonably jealous.

"I'm Jack Snow," he said.

"Lily Delacy Shanahan. And this," she indicated her hound, "is Nala." She nodded and then pressed both fists to her hips, regarding him as if he had just tracked mud onto her clean kitchen floor. "You're shivering."

Her expression was so dark he found himself resisting the urge to tremble, succeeding momentarily, before the jerking spasms sent his teeth knocking together again.

"Follow me." She tugged at the dog's harness and set the cart in motion.

"What about my things?"

She turned away from Jack and let loose an ear-splitting whistle, which brought a scrappy young man to her. "Watch these." She told him as she pressed something into his palm.

"You betcha," said the lad.

Lily looked back at him and then set off again, bringing less than half of his gear along. He stood for a minute torn between following and remaining with the rest of his belongings. Could this be an elaborate scheme to rob him?

In the end, his shivering got the better of him and he hurried to catch up. They followed a hard-packed trail up over the rocky beach. Everywhere, men stacked bags and boxes of their belongings. Some had even staked their tents right there where the rock met the scrappy willow. As they continued, the hum of eager conversation and shouted orders drowned out the crashing waves that had almost destroyed him.

The road widened as they crossed through the willows. Her dog strained to pull his things up the incline. Lily glanced back at him.

"Well? Push!"

He scowled, far more used to giving orders than taking them. But he did as she bade, and together, he and the hound managed to crest the rise. The dog received all of the praise, while he did not even gain a backward glance. He frowned, more at the realization that he wanted her attention than from the lack of it. That would not do. He refused to become bewitched by a little firebrand like this. He was stuck with her, but he didn't have to like it.

Ahead lay Dyea, a large tent city with stripped logs for street posts and only a few timber structures. Cold, dark mud turned the streets to quagmire and crept up the canvas that passed for buildings here. Some of the tents were large enough to hold a circus, but instead of sawdust and prancing white ponies, they held rows of rough-hewn tables with hungry men eating in makeshift restaurants. They passed Brackett's Trading Post, singular for its two stories and five glass windows, though no one had yet painted the exterior, which had already weathered to a dark gray. A steady stream of stampeders picked their way along with horses and mules. He wished he could trade places with any one of them.

Each of the tents had a stovepipe poking from the roof like the stem of an apple. He was glad he had one himself, a very light efficient stove that burned nearly five hours on just two split logs. Lily turned down this road and up the next until he was thoroughly lost in the maze of identical canvases.

She stopped before an unremarkable tent that looked hardly big enough for one, let alone two.

"This is it," she said.

He frowned.

"You're not much of a poker player, I imagine," she said.

He glanced at her, trying to understand the cryptic comment but she only laughed and patted him amiably on the shoulder, then began unloading his gear. She was so petit. How would she endure the journey? In a few moments they had his belongings stacked beside the tent flap.

"You have clothes in here?" She indicated the pile.

He stared in mute astonishment as he realized his duffel with all his personal belongings lay back with the unknown lad. He could not fathom the oversight. Jack needed to do better if he was to succeed. The Yukon would be no more forgiving than the banks back home had been. He gritted his clattering teeth.

There was no way to recapture what was lost. His only choice was to start again.

His mother disagreed. This expedition terrified her. She had told him that having lost her husband she could not bear the thought of losing her only son, as well. It pained him to worry her and he did fear what would become of them should he not return. Were it up to his mother, he'd be safe at home looking for a wife with a fortune. The thought turned his stomach. He would be his own man, despite the risks. Her latest telegram had reached him in Seattle, begging him to reconsider. He'd written that he was pressing on. He'd earn his fortune and return to have his pick of the New York debutants. He'd have his old life back or return like a whipped dog.

He looked up to find her staring at him.

She shook her head in dismay. "Go on in and strip out of those things. Take a blanket off my bed and heat the coffee. It's in the pot. You do know how to rake coals and start a fire?"

"Of course."

She made a harrumphing sound as if she did not believe it. It occurred to him suddenly that he might not be her ideal partner, either, though he could not see her objection. She turned the dog cart and stopped. "Leave the flap open or your crates will likely walk away on you. You have a pistol?"

"Not on me."

"I find they do more good when they are carried

in plain sight." She patted the handle of her Colt. "You're not at Yale now, college boy. There are thieves everywhere here."

With that she set the cart in motion, as he wondered if she were among the thieves. Was this even her tent?

"Princeton, actually."

She shrugged and continued on.

He shouted after her. "And how do you know I went to college?"

She called back without stopping. "Only an educated man would be fool enough to carry a crate of books to the Yukon. Might make good tinder, I suppose."

He looked at the broken crate, lid askew. On top lay his copy of *The Notebooks of Leonardo da Vinci,* edited by Jean Paul Richter. The woman acted as if it were a box of dumbbells or some other useless fodder.

Eventually his shivering forced him into retreat, but he kept the tent flap up. The woman was shrewd with the kind of knowledge that did not come from a classroom, he'd give her that.

The inside of her tent was much more spartan than he had anticipated. In his experience, women shared a pack rat's propensity for dragging home bits of glitter and fluff. Lily Delacy Shanahan's tent looked as if it belonged to a new cadet. Her bed was made with sharp corners. Her wood supply was ample and well away from the stove. She had a small, neat kitchen area all set up, including the coffeepot. He sloshed the contents and found it still half-full. Jack stoked the coals and added kindling, sighing in relief as the flames lapped around the slender branches. She had one crate beside the bed and a sack, sewn from a piece of canvas, hanging from a tent post. He shrugged at the oddness of her private quarters. His shivering made it difficult to unbutton his sodden coat. Jack's trembling fingers looked ghostly white from lack of blood as he wrestled with his sweater and flannel shirt. Then he peeled out of his union suit, bringing it down to his waist. Only when he was holding his soaked garments did he notice the clothesline stretched tight over the stove. He added *organized* to her list of attributes as he threw his things over the line and then held his hands out to the stove. It was no good. The shaking was worse and his skin was as puckered-up as a plucked chicken's. A glance at his nail beds startled him. The blue tinge had him doing as she had instructed, removing the red Hudson's Bay blanket from her bed and wrapping it over his shoulders. The coarse wool grazed his damp skin as her scent reached him and he paused to inhale—cinnamon. The shivering brought him close to the stove. He set the coffeepot on the top and then jumped up and down until his numb feet began to tingle.

A few minutes later the coffeepot steamed and

he poured himself a hot mug. He inhaled the aroma and hummed in pleasure.

"Take off your boots!" Lily harped from the street.

Jack nearly dropped his coffee. He glanced down at the ground and saw it was hard-packed earth, making her request totally illogical.

"You can't track dirt onto dirt," he said, thinking that reasoning with a woman was as productive as explaining physics to a cocker spaniel.

"Your feet are wet. You have to warm them or you'll get frostbite."

She was correct again, though he wouldn't say so aloud. She knelt before him, muttering as her agile fingers worked the laces from the eyelets. Then she slapped his calf as if he were a horse needing his hooves picked clean. He shifted his weight, giving her his foot and trying very hard not to drop the hot coffee on her head. She pulled and the boot came away.

"I was about to get to those," he muttered. *Just as soon as I can feel my fingers again.*

She cast him a displeased glance. "And leave a toe or two here in Dyea? Now that I've got you, I'll be damned if I'll let your toes turn black."

"It's barely below freezing."

She ignored that and returned her attention to his feet. He'd only wanted to warm his hands a moment first and then she'd blown in like a March wind. His jaws now tapped like the signal key of a telegraph.

"The other," she ordered and repeated the process.

But this time the blanket slipped to the floor. He placed the cup on the top of the stove and then stooped to recover it, just as she did the same.

They nearly banged heads and came up standing face-to-face with the blanket stretched between them. It was only then that he realized she was staring wide-eyed at his naked torso. His impulse was to grab the blanket and cover himself, but something about her startled expression stayed him. Her cheeks flushed and her lips separated as she inhaled. He recognized the look of carnal desire and couldn't move now if he tried, for she had arrested him. His entire body tensed. Her azure eyes lifted from his chest to stare up at him. She inched closer.

The cold that had gripped him like an icy fist melted in the heat of her gaze, warming him inside and out.

She lifted her free hand and reached for him. His heart galloped into a wild pulsing rhythm, sending fountains of blood to his groin. Dear Lord in heaven, she managed to arouse him without so much as a touch. The touch came an instant later when she used her index finger to stroke his chest, as if skimming cream from a bowl.

"You're cold," she whispered, her voice a second caress.

His mind filled with all the ways she could warm him and he took an aggressive step in her direction, lifting his hands to capture her shoulders, needing to bring her against him. But she resisted and he let go. She stumbled back, now gripping the blanket with both hands. Her expression had changed in that instant, going from an open invitation to one of ill-concealed horror. Her fists clenched, holding the coarse wool before her as if it were some kind of magic shield that would protect her from him.

It wouldn't.

"We're not that kind of partners," she said.

His brain knew it, but his body was still beating the order to advance. He listened to his body, stepping forward, reaching again in an effort to recapture what was already lost, that heat she had given him with her flashing eyes and that one single touch.

She stepped back. "No."

Even with his blood pounding through his ears like hoofbeats, he was gentleman enough to understand that. He halted. His current befuddlement had nothing whatsoever to do with the cold. No, this was all to do with this woman. He wanted her.

She shook out the blanket and then held it up.

He turned and she wrapped the red wool about his shoulders, her arms encircling his neck for just an instant before she retreated again.

Jack turned, now cloaked in his cape. She blew out a breath as one does after a narrow escape. But she had not escaped yet. Why had she done it? Had his nakedness precipitated her rash action? It gave him a sense of power he'd never felt before and filled his mind with possibilities.

"Lily?" He had no idea what to say beyond that. How did a man express such a physical desire to a woman he had met scarcely two hours earlier? He couldn't. His heartbeat returned to a more normal pace and the erection, which had sprung to action like a soldier to the signal to charge, now returned to at-ease. He began to shiver again.

"Drink your coffee," she instructed.

He didn't. Instead he held her gaze.

"Why did you touch me like that?"

Chapter Three

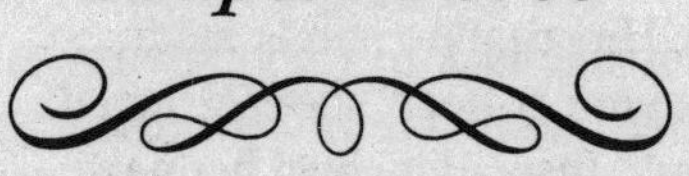

Why *had* she touched him like that? Lily was at a loss to explain herself. Clearly she'd lost her damned mind. The bold action brought to mind her mother's warning. *If you need a man, then take one, but don't give him your heart, Lily, for he'll only break it with his leaving.* Lily had decided that she'd not be needing a man in that way. Men propositioned her, of course, one or two had even tried to take what they wanted. But she had been unaffected, until now. In all her years she had never reached out and stroked a man as if he were her pet cat.

Seeing all that muscle did something to her thinking. She'd known on the beach that she was attracted to him, but she had told herself she could control her desire. Now the demons of doubt plagued her. What if the only difference between her and her ma was that, until today, she had not yet met the right sort of temptation?

She shivered. If Jack Snow was her weakness, she should break the deal that he so clearly wanted broken and send him off this very minute. She weighed the risk of being hurt against the possibility of ever again finding a partner as strong as this one.

What terrible luck to find a man who made her belly flutter like a flag in a windstorm. It would lead her to a bad end. But wasn't this exactly how her mother described it—the irresistible pull of one to the other. Carrie Delacy had been unable to resist big, handsome charmers who had not a penny in their pockets or the least inclination to work. Lily stared at her partner and stilled at her realization. Was Jack just like them? Would he leave her, too?

"Lily?" he asked, waiting for her to say something.

Her stomach no longer trembled. Now it tightened with that sick feeling that she would not be able to control this desire that stood between them like a living thing. Why was he so handsome? Even with his whiskers coming in and his hair falling over his eyes, she had the devil's own time not to take what he offered. She didn't want to be hurt, used like her mother and then abandoned by careless men.

Her mother wanted more for her daughter than this. One child, then another and before Lily knew it, she'd be leaning over the same washboard wondering where her life had gone wrong. Right here was where. It was exactly what her mother had *not* wanted for her.

That realization struck her hard. Yield to him and she'd be just like her mother, stuck in these mudflats forever, hauling freight and darning socks, while Jack waltzed away to have the adventure she coveted.

"No, thank you," she said aloud. "I'm heading out, so get your things off my cart."

He had to abandon the blanket and pull up his wet union suit, but he did as she asked, unloading his gear and stacking it with the rest. She did not look back as she hurried Nala away.

On the beach she paid another hauler to take the rest of his gear to her tent. She earned several more fares, staying longer than customary to stay clear of him. Soon that would be an impossibility.

Late in the day, she came upon a man struggling with his crates and suitcases. He was thin, dark-haired and wore a small white fringed apron beneath his gray vest. She offered her cart, but he had nothing with which to pay her.

"I'll pay you twice that in gold when I reach Dawson."

Lily smiled at his pluck. There was a good chance he'd never reach his destination. Many turned back after seeing the Chilkoot Pass and many more drowned in the rivers. Even if he survived, he might not be one of the lucky ones that staked a profitable claim.

"Cash."

"I can't pay it, missus." His face grew pink with shame that Lily understood from personal experience.

Lily sighed. It was not the first time she'd hauled a load for nothing but a man's gratitude. Still she had enough to fill her pot, so where was the harm?

"All right. Load it on," she said.

He did so and soon they were on their way up the beach.

"I'm Amos Luritz."

Lily introduced herself and her dog.

"I was a tailor in Brooklyn."

Lily smiled.

"I made this coat."

"Very nice."

"Men's clothing, repairs and alterations, but I do make all my daughters' dresses. I have two beautiful daughters, Sasha and Cora. They're with my in-laws until I can make my fortune."

"Then we'd best get you to town."

"I could make you a dress when we get to Dawson, in exchange for your trouble."

"Oh, that's not necessary, Mr. Luritz."

"You can't make a living giving away your work."

"True. But I did quite well today."

"I'll make you the most beautiful dress in Dawson."

"I fear you'll be too busy digging for gold."

He nodded at this. "Would you take one of my nuggets?"

"That would be lovely, Mr. Luritz. But I'll likely have so many of my own, I'll not need yours." She winked at him and he chuckled.

"You're a good lady, missus."

She compared this greenhorn to Jack. Two men, both without means, only this one had a clear and useful profession instead of several hundred pounds of baggage. If she had come across Amos first, would he now be her partner? She wished he was, for she felt no inclination toward him. What was so different between this man and the one she had chosen?

She pondered that mystery as Amos trudged along beside her on the half-mile trip to Dyea, yammering all the way about the nuggets he would find and the money he needed to open his own tailor shop in Brooklyn. She stopped him from showing her a photo of his wife and daughters. Lily didn't want to have their images in her mind should something happen to this brave little tailor.

She worked until the sun hung low in the sky and all the arrivals had made their way to Dyea. Days were growing short now, adding to her anxiousness to be gone from this place.

She stopped at the log home of Yaahl, the Chilkat

Indian whose wife, Diinaan, fed Nala in exchange for Lily's accounting work. The couple and their family carried loads over the pass to the upper end of Lake Lindeman. Diinaan carried only seventy-five pounds a trip, a white man's load, she called it, but her husband could carry two hundred pounds at twenty-six cents a pound. It was Lily who had encouraged them to increase the asking fee from eighteen cents as the stampeders rushed in to Dyea.

"I found a partner," she said, sitting beside Diinaan on the bench outside the door.

Nala was busy wolfing down the mixture of rice, dried salmon and bacon grease.

"Oh, so you going now soon. Yes?"

"Yes. I'll need to pick up the sled and buy dried fish for Nala. Plus I'd like to hear anything more you can tell me about the trail."

"Yes, I tell you much trail news all the way to top lakes. I miss your good advice and account…" Her words fell off.

"Accounting."

"Yes."

Lily had taught Diinaan bookkeeping in exchange for a sled, that for a time there, she had feared she would never need.

"It's important to keep track so you aren't cheated."

They exchanged a smile. Lily would miss Diinaan

because, although they were separated by race and culture, at heart they were the same.

Nala began licking the bowl until it spun like a top, the metal bottom ringing against the rock. Lily called her off. It was time to face what she had avoided for much of the day—the man, her partner, waiting in her tent. Her insides went tense as she returned to her tent and Jack.

She reached her temporary home a few minutes later, hopeful that Mr. Snow had dried his clothing and was now wearing both a shirt and trousers. She called out and waited until he shouted a hello, then she drew a large breath of icy air and ducked inside. Lily gasped as her gaze darted about—for in a matter of mere hours the man had turned her orderly home into chaos. Every crate had been opened and the shavings scattered about. Piles of sheet metal and pipe covered her bed, tools and gadgets of unknown usefulness were strewn over her kitchen table. And there in the midst of the chaos sat Mr. Snow, on her bed beside her oil lamp, calmly polishing some kind of round gauge with a bit of white cotton, that she recognized belatedly as one of her embroidered handkerchiefs as he whistled softly to himself.

Her jaw dropped at the sight, her nerves and restless anticipation forgotten amid the anarchy. Lily narrowed her eyes upon him and he stilled. The whistling ceased as silence stretched.

Her voice was a soft exhalation bubbling with

indignation. "Isn't this exactly what comes from letting a man into your home?"

He flushed and rose, staring down at the handkerchief and then hiding it behind his back.

"The packing was all soaked. I have to dry the metal or it will rust."

"This is the most useless bundle of nonsense I've ever seen a man haul from Seattle. Even the piano that went through here had more value than this lot."

"No, it will be useful."

"For what, building a metal boat? Are you daft, man? You can't haul two tons of pig iron to Dawson."

"It weighs only 820 pounds."

She turned in a circle, dismay now rushing in to fill the void left by her shock. "And not one sled or rope or scrap of food or canvas," she muttered. She fixed him with a cold stare. "Where are your mining tools?"

"Already cleaned and dried. There." He pointed to a stack of crates. "Carpentry, mining and sheet metal."

"And what are you planning to eat, shoe leather?"

"I have dried lentils, rice, bacon and coffee."

She sighed in relief. Nala whined and Lily was grateful for the distraction of removing the dog's harness. Once finished, she turned to Jack Snow.

"When I come back, I'd best be able to sit on my bed."

She dropped the canvas flap and stepped out into

the cold night. What the devil had she been thinking to bring him into her home?

Lily snapped her fingers and Nala appeared, trotting beside her as she picked her way through the mud to the saloon, where she took her meals. The men shouted a greeting as she entered. She waved as she went to the back, where Taps had her dinner waiting. The barkeep had been a bugler in the army, thus his name.

"I'll need a second plate to go."

Taps stilled. "Did you find a partner, Lil?"

"That's so," she piped with a bravado she did not feel. Lily was used to feigning grit and a cheerful disposition, for who wanted to listen to a dour performer? But sometimes she wished she were back in her mother's kitchen making apricot preserves. *No sense in looking back at what's lost,* her mother would say. *Forward, girls, forward.*

"Fine, fine," said Taps, adjusting his greasy hat.

"And he's a strapping big one, too," she added as much to herself as to him. It wasn't all bad, was it? She'd gotten a man and could head out now. Lily tamped down her rising panic.

"But he's got only one leg?"

Her laugh sounded hollow, but no one seemed to notice but herself. She'd not let them see her anxiety over her new partner. "So far as I can see his only fault is that he's a man."

Taps nodded. "Then you'd best sleep with that revolver under your pillow."

Her smile slipped. "Don't worry about me." She glanced about and located the closest stampeder. "George! Kiss me."

George's bushy eyebrows lifted but he did not argue. He took one step toward her and wrapped his arms about her waist.

Nala leapt to her feet, bared her teeth and gave a menacing growl. George lifted his hands in surrender, backing away.

The others laughed.

"She's better at defending me than my dear old dad," said Lily, pressing a hand to her chest. In truth her father hadn't given a fig about her and had left them like the rest. What was it about her that made them all go? Her mother insisted it wasn't Lily's fault, but why then?

Taps slid her dinner onto the bar and Lily quickly finished her only meal of the day, using her bread as a sponge to capture the last of the gravy. Then she patted her middle and allowed two men to boost her up to the bar. She began with a hearty rendition of "My Darling Clementine," followed by several rousing drinking tunes that the men could sing along with, then turned to some sweet love songs and finished with "Pretty Saro." That one made many a greenhorn weep. Her hour done, she climbed down from the bar, gathered up the second plate of food and headed back to her partner.

When she reached her tent she found he'd packed up the crates and bags of gear. Only a few items of clothing still remained on the line and he sat in the single chair beside the stove with a leather journal clutched to his chest and his head thrown back as he snored softly.

He'd turned down the wick of her oil lamp. That and the glow from the small window in the potbelly stove made his skin a warm, rosy color. Lily studied him again. Asleep, Jack Snow was still handsome, but the threat was gone. Now she felt only an inexplicable tenderness and the need to brush the locks of hair from his forehead. She reached and then stopped herself by clenching her fist. No, not that way. That was the way to build attachments that would make his leaving more painful. She sealed herself against him in an effort to protect her bruised heart from further battering.

She was freezing from her walk across the tent town. It might be only October, but the temperature dropped at night like a rock tossed from a cliff.

Nala whined.

"Shh," said Lily as she moved forward to place Jack's supper on the flat round top of the stove to warm. As she straightened she caught the unfamiliar scent of him—sawdust, leather and the musty smell of the sea. The heat of the stove penetrated the frosty cold that seemed to cling to her skin, making her linger near him.

It wasn't his full open mouth or the straight line of his nose, it wasn't those feathery black eyelashes brushing his cheek that drew her. No, it was only the stove. She needed the heat, that was all, and tonight the cast iron was throwing more than usual, wasn't it?

"Damn, it's him again," she whispered.

Nala nudged Jack's hand with her big wet nose and he startled awake to find himself surrounded with Lily on the left and Nala on the right. He clutched the armrests of the chair for an instant and the book slid to his thighs. His eyes grew wide and then he relaxed, resting his hand on Nala's head and scratching her behind the ears.

Lily didn't know which shocked her more, that Nala had sought attention from this stranger or that he had given it without thought. So much for her watchdog. Lily felt Nala's betrayal like a pinprick in her heart.

She'd seen several men try to approach Nala, hands out, voices soothing, but she had snapped at them all. Lily stared at Jack Snow. What made him different?

He stretched and then cast her that beguiling smile. The man could coax cider from an apple. Lily frowned.

"Must have dozed off." He glanced about. "Got it all stowed, partner."

Partner. She liked the sound of it on his lips. Lily dropped her gaze and pointed to the stove. "I brought supper."

Jack's smile broadened. "Excellent. I'm so hungry I could eat a horse." He thumped Nala on the ribs. "Present company excluded."

Nala's tail thudded against the chair back.

What was happening here?

"Eat your supper."

He drew the plate to his lap and looked about. It was in that instant she realized she had no utensils. So she brought him the large spoon she used to measure coffee and handed it over. His fingers brushed hers and she stilled at the startling sensation running up her arm like the feet of tiny birds.

She backed away, sitting on the bed behind him. He turned his chair so that he faced her but he did not fall upon his food. He must be hungry, yet still he hesitated.

"Go on," she urged.

He pursed his lips. "You've eaten?"

It seemed hours ago. She smiled and nodded. "Yes—eat."

He waited a moment longer and then attacked the beans and rice as she poured him a cup of coffee, black. When she set it on the stove she found him laying the three strips of thick bacon into the bread, which he folded in half. He finished the sandwich in five large bites.

"Where did you find Nala?" asked Jack, resting a large hand on her dog's wide head.

Lily smiled before she answered and for a moment Jack forgot the question. Did she even know how lovely she was?

"When I first laid eyes on her, she was in the jaws of an alley cat that was big as a lion. She was a pup no bigger than this." Lily indicated a distance of six or seven inches between her palms. "But I chased that cat down and made her drop the pup. She gave me this for my trouble." Lily pointed to the little puncture below her right eye, the only flaw in her beautiful skin. "Tried to take my eye out. And Nala's still got the scars on her head where that cat bit into her." She patted the dog's ribs affectionately.

Jack scratched the dog's head feeling the bumps on her scalp.

"I feel them," he said.

Lily nodded and continued her tale. "I carried her home in the pocket of my coat. Can you imagine? She was so tiny, her eyes weren't even open. Had to feed her milk from my finger, and it was no small trouble stealing milk each morning, I can tell you."

Jack frowned at the thought of Lily having to steal milk. He found himself wondering what Lily had endured in her youth and how she had managed to come out so well. True she was guarded, but who could blame her? Likely she had seen enough of life's troubles to be streetwise and was apt to be much more astute in that regard than he was.

Nala sat beside his chair, eyes closed as she enjoyed the stove's heat.

Jack lowered his plate, still sticky with the gravy and a few stray grains of rice, to the floor. Nala needed no second invitation. Her pink tongue lapped the pewter until it seemed spotless.

Lily retrieved the plate and set it aside.

"Was that good?" said Jack to Nala in a friendly tone that made Lily's stomach flutter.

"She's not your dog." Her voice came out harsher than she'd intended.

His eyes rounded. "I'm sorry. I should have asked permission before feeding her. It's just. Well. I had a black dog once."

"What kind?"

"Teddy was a chow. When his eyes got cloudy, we just stretched a rope in the back, like a clothesline. He loved to run and knew exactly when to stop. He was a good boy." His sad, wistful expression made her sorry for her sharp words.

Lily extended her hand and Nala moved to sit beside her cot. "Do you have a tent?"

He nodded.

She tried to turn her mind to business, instead of the crisp, dark, curling hair that showed above the open two buttons of his union suit.

"We'll need to compare lists of gear to see what we still need and what can be left behind."

His brow wrinkled as if he couldn't understand leaving things. Did he even know what was involved in this journey?

"Yes, all right," he said.

They talked late into the night, her new partner taking notes and making lists of the items they had, needed or would abandon. He was educated, but lacked practicality, as she had feared. She failed to get him to agree to leave the metal behind, nor would he share the utility of this load, except to say it would be "the practical application of a working model" whatever that meant.

She liked that it was practical, at least in his eyes and since she would not be carrying it, she said no more. She shared what she had learned from the Chilkat Indians and he spoke of what he had gleaned from newspapers, maps and geography texts. But in truth, neither of them had seen the trail that would take three to six months to cross, stretching over five hundred miles, first through the narrow gap between great mountains and then down lakes and rivers that became the Yukon River, which would finally carry them to the goldfields in Dawson City.

Exhaustion took hold and they grew silent.

He gazed at the woman who only looked more beautiful by firelight. She was an astute planner, he'd give her that, but that was not why his gaze lingered on the graceful curve of her neck and the soft wisps of dark hair that caressed her skin.

"Why did you come?" she asked.

Jack snapped his gaze back to hers, shaking from his reverie. He was uncomfortable with the personal question.

"For the same reason as other men. I came to test myself and my ideas."

She laughed. The musical sound made his palms sweat. He clamped them to the arms of the chair.

"You're a strange sort, Jack, and the first I've come across wanting to test ideas. The rest of them come to get rich. I've come for that, too, but I've also come for the adventure."

He leaned forward, drawn by the energetic sparkle in her eyes. Lily's thinly veiled accent marked her as lower-class Irish. Not the sort of woman he must have to regain his social position. But he didn't rule out an affair, if she was willing.

She'd be used to hard work, at least.

Once upon a time, he would not have even spoken with someone the likes of her, yet here they were—partners. What would she say if she knew that the only labor he'd done involved rowing on crew and playing for Princeton's football team? They'd won the national championship last year against Lafayette. He wondered how they were faring this season without him. He thought of his teammates. Many would be graduating without him come spring. He'd been too ashamed to say goodbye, didn't want them to know of his family's ruin, but now that he thought of them he wondered how many others had lost everything when the bottom dropped out of the market. Still, he couldn't tell them, not even Eric, his roommate and closest friend. He was too humiliated and found it easier to wall away his sorrow. Sins of the father. His chin sank a little closer to his chest as he wished he had Eric along instead of this lovely, resolute little woman. His head nodded forward, surprising him. He snapped upright.

"You have a bedroll?" she asked.

He nodded.

"Stretch it out beside the cot."

He was wide awake now. He'd never shared a room with a woman, and just thinking of sleeping in the same tent as Lily Delacy Shanahan aroused more than his mind.

"But what will people think?"

"People? You mean the raggedy greenhorns sleeping on the beach or the swindlers in town? Here, men care only for themselves. Plus, I don't give a fig what they think or what they say. I answer to no one but myself. What you should be worried about is what I think, because if you so much as lay a finger on me in the night, I'll shoot you through the heart."

That said, she laid her hand on the grip of her revolver and eyed him. He nodded his understanding, but could not help but notice the quick rise and fall of her chest. It didn't match the cool look in her eyes. Something didn't fit, but he said no more as he retrieved his blanket roll.

"I'm off to use the necessary," she said.

"Is there one?"

"Not really." She smiled. "Come, Nala."

Jack had his bedding open and had rolled his coat for a pillow when he heard Lily screaming just beyond the canvas flaps.

"Let her go!"

Jack leapt to his feet and hurtled out of the tent.

Chapter Four

Jack skidded to a halt in the muddy street, dark now, except for the glow of lamps and candles shielded by canvas, but he saw them instantly, tussling in the narrow thoroughfare. He took in the scene in a fraction of a second. Two men—one straining to hold Nala's harness as the dog jumped and barked in a vain effort to reach her mistress, the other with Lily's wrists pinned before him, preventing her from reaching her weapon.

Something inside Jack snapped. One minute he was on guard and cognizant and the next he was a wild animal tearing and punching. He grabbed the man gripping Lily by the back of his pants and the collar of his dark coat and lifted him into the air. Her attacker writhed and kicked, for just an instant before Jack threw him onto a stack of firewood, scattering the neat pile. The man lay unmoving amid the strewn cordage. Then he turned on the one holding Nala. The ruffian had taken his eyes off the dog, his jaw dropping open as he witnessed Jack's approach. In that instant, Nala turned and sank her teeth into the man's forearm. Jack heard the bone snap. The fellow gave a shriek of pain, but the hound did not let go and began a violent shaking of her head. The man howled in agony.

The idea of forcing the dog to release him never even crossed Jack's mind. He was too deep into the all-consuming rage. He added his weight to the dog's attack, punching the man's face with all he had. The attacker dropped to the ground and fell silent. Only then did Nala unlock her jaws.

Jack turned back to the other man, still unconscious and then returned to the one lying face-down in the mud. Lily moved beside Jack. Instinctively he grasped her around the waist, dragging her tight to his body, holding her in the protection of his arms, his eyes scanning for any remaining threat.

The haze of red receded by degrees and Jack saw the circle of spectators, gawking at him as if he were a madman.

Lily spoke first. "They tried to steal my dog."

A short, stocky man stepped forward. His face bristled with gray whiskers and tobacco juice glistened on his chin. "Jonathan, get some rope to tie these two." Next he pointed to a man who stood stoop-shouldered in muddy boots. "Bobby, get that horsewhip of yours."

Jack suddenly realized what was happening. Vigilante justice—his stomach cramped at the thought. Disapproval filled him. Men could not simply take the law into their own hands. Then his mind flashed to an image of Lily struggling vainly for escape. The fury overtook him again and he decided they deserved far worse.

"Call the authorities!" someone shouted.

There was a moment's silence and then men guffawed.

"Authorities?" said the stocky man. "There ain't no law 'til you reach the Canadian border."

Lily had told him as much. But he hadn't really understood it until now. He'd never lived in a place where people made up the rules as they went along.

This tent town was an illusion. All these men were gathered only to ready themselves for the push to Dawson. Then the entire town would vanish and remake itself inland. They were like ants, scurrying in the mud.

"What will you do with them?" Jack asked, longing to bloody his fists on the men's faces again.

"Whip 'em. Then we'll run them out of Dyea."

Jack glanced down to see Lily's strained, brave little face and pulled her even closer, shaken at the realization that he would have killed for her.

Lily still clung to his middle, staring up at him in

astonishment. Was that horror or a kind of newfound respect? The need to protect her warred with the desire to claim her as his. Jack slipped one hand up to tangle in her hair, taking possession of her.

She pushed off him like a swimmer from the side of a pool and stepped back.

Her words came to him again. *We're not that kind of partners.*

"Damn," he muttered and let her go.

The two men were dragged off, feet-first. Jack looked at the distance he had thrown the first man and could not quite believe it.

Nala jumped up on Lily, muddying her fine crimson coat. But she hugged the dog, resting her head against the thick scruff of the mongrel's neck.

"Good girl, Nala. That's my girl." Her hound dropped to all fours. But Lily just followed her, squatting in the street before him. She straightened at last, coming close enough for him to breathe in her fragrance of cinnamon and musk again. She placed one hand flat on his chest, reminding him of her earlier caress.

The small action nearly stopped his heart and made it surprisingly difficult to draw a full breath.

"That was very brave," she whispered. She stepped back and laced her fingers together then wrung her hands. "Thank you."

He blinked. "You're welcome."

"Who's your man, Lil?" asked a ruddy-faced gent with a fine crop of hair sprouting from each nostril.

She lifted a hand, presenting him to the group of curiosity seekers.

"Boys, meet Jack Snow, my new partner."

Jack braced, waiting for someone to recognize his surname.

A ripple went through the crowd, but after a moment he realized it was not for the reason he feared. Perhaps he had finally found a place where he could be who he was now instead of who he had been.

Some of the male bystanders looked amused, while others simply stared, slack-jawed. A few stepped forward to shake his hand or clap him on the shoulder. He breathed again when he realized they did not know him or his family. The scandal that had blanketed the pages of the papers in New York meant nothing to these men. No one knew. No one cared—no one but him.

Lily's smile was bright and her laughter contagious. She seemed the darling of the street with many admirers already. It took a long while for the men to return to their tents.

At last, Nala had had enough and ducked between the flaps and out of sight. Lily laughed and followed her example.

"He staying in your tent?" asked a man with a gray-streaked beard.

She turned and rested a hand on her hip, looking down her nose at the man. "Your partner sleep in your tent, Bill?"

"Well, yeah, but..."

"But what?" she asked, daring him to say another word.

He rubbed the toe of his boot in the mud. "It's different."

She laughed. "Get your mind out of the gutter, boys." She aimed her finger at them. "All of you. The only female Jack will be sleeping with tonight is Nala."

Jack pressed his lips together as the others laughed. With that she sniffed and disappeared into the tent after her hound. Jack suddenly worried over his bedding and the muddy dog that preceded him into the tent. He hurried to follow.

Just as he feared, Nala had dragged his bedroll into a nice muddy mess on which she was now curled. Lily ordered her dog up and handed Jack his bedding, now streaked with dirt.

"Don't worry. If you plan on being a miner, everything you own will soon look like this."

Jack accepted the grimy blankets with dismay that lasted only until Lily's next words.

"Let's get some sleep."

Jack stood as if petrified as she sat on her cot and removed her boots with a button hook, carefully placing the worn leather beneath her bed. Then she peeled out of her coat, revealing a neat blue woolen bodice and matching skirt.

She began to brush the mud off her coat.

"Do you have a sweetheart, Mr. Snow?"

He thought he'd prefer jumping back in the icy inlet waters than tell her about his former fiancée, Nancy Tinsen.

"Never stayed with one long enough to call her that."

Lily pulled a face, and then unbuttoned her bodice. She stopped when the garment gapped, revealing the fine, soft swell of her breasts above the corset that cinched her in the middle.

"Here is what will happen. You'll excuse yourself and go for a walk. When you come back the lamp will be out and I'll be in bed. If you try to crawl under my blankets, I'll use my pistol."

"What if you try to crawl under mine?"

That stopped her. She gaped a moment and then laughed. "Well now, then I suppose you have your choice to throw me out or keep me."

"I'd keep you." He held her long stare. She looked away first.

Her voice seemed breathless when she next spoke. "I can't see that happening."

Now it was his turn to smile. "Can't you?"

He was gratified to see her flush. So he hadn't imagined the pull between them. He didn't want a full-time woman, not when he was still bruised and battered from his failed engagement. But he wasn't beyond taking what a woman offered.

"You can take that walk now."

Jack lifted the flap but she called him back.

"And Jack?"

He turned, thinking her beautiful in the lamplight.

"Hmm?"

"Thank you for tonight."

He pinned her with a steady stare. "What are partners for."

Then he left her, before the temptation to stay caused him to do something he'd regret. He paused beyond the tent, waiting for his eyes to adjust. He could scarcely make out the dark silhouette of the figure across the road.

"Toss you out already?" he asked.

Jack could see little beyond the glowing tip of a cigarette, but he made his way over.

"So it seems." He walked to the man who offered his tobacco pouch. "No, thanks."

The man took another puff. "Thing about canvas is that voices carry. I guess folks know just about everything about their neighbors here, 'cept they aren't neighbors, since folks come and go by the minute. Nobody really cares for anyone but themselves—and their partners, of course. The rest is all entertainment."

"Why you telling me this?"

"Just to thank you for livening up this little corner of the swamp. I'm George Suffern."

Jack shook his hand.

"When you two pushing up the Chilkoot?"

"Sooner is better," said Jack.

"I suppose. The steamers will keep coming until the passages freeze. Father Winter hits early in the mountains. Maybe best to stay down here, then head up come spring."

Jack sat on the crate beside him. "No, you're wrong. Best to get up to Lake Bennett and spend the winter building your boat. Then you'll be in position when the ice break-up comes. From there it's all downhill to Dawson."

"Through rapids and lakes filled with more mosquito larva than fish."

Jack laughed. "That's why it's an adventure. A test of a man's metal."

"And what about Lily? She's your partner now, so it's your lookout to see she gets to Dawson. Big responsibility. I reckon that'll test your metal more than the Golden Stairs or the White Horse Rapids."

Jack winced as he chafed against their bargain. If he were a different kind of man he'd leave her behind and never look back. But, unlike his father, Jack valued his word and kept his promises. So he would attend to his responsibilities, but it annoyed him that he'd somehow fallen into the worst of all situations, giving him all of the responsibilities of keeping a woman with none of the benefits.

He glanced at the tent in time to see the light extinguish. Lily was now climbing into her narrow bed alone—such a shame. Jack stood, drawn by the perfect image of Lily's fine luminous skin glowing in the moonlight. His throat went dry as he took a step.

George cleared his throat, making Jack recall his presence.

He stopped and gave the man his attention. He didn't like the man's mocking smile.

"My daddy used to say that you should never tie an eagle to a plow horse, because the arrangement won't be good for either of them. I'm afraid, son, you've got yourself in just such a situation."

Jack wondered if he were the eagle or the horse. But he'd heard enough lectures about the folly of this venture from his mother who had advised he stay put, lower his expectations in the marriage market and seek a bride outside their former circles. It might still come to that, but first he would try and be his own man. Jack thought his mother might even admire his wish to restore them to their rightful place, if she could only see past her fears of losing him forever. He knew the risks here. The dangers were real, but they were real back there. What hope did he have, cloaked in scandal, flat broke, with no degree and no prospects? Save the one his mother had found him.

He cringed. Here, at least, he stood a chance to be his own man instead of having to marry a woman he did not even know. But if he failed he might be forced to that to provide for his mother and sister. The thought left a bitter taste in his mouth.

I'm sorry, Mother, I've got to try, he thought, placing a hand over his heart and her telegram that had found him in Seattle.

His greatest fear was dying up here and leaving his mother and younger sister dependent on the charity of his aunt and uncle.

"You two sure are a mismatched team." George blew a smoke ring. "Maybe you should…she told me that before this she'd never been more than five blocks in any direction. Don't think she's prepared for this, though she knows her own mind, I suppose."

Jack felt a chill run down his back at the realization that Lily knew nothing of the dangers of this wild place. She'd shown tonight how ill-equipped she was, nearly losing her dog to ruffians. Somehow he'd been taken in by her bravado, but now it suddenly became clear that his job would involve more than carrying her to Dawson. He'd have to defend her from other men as well. Could he do it? He had to.

Jack lifted his collar but felt no warmer as he realized he was not the eagle, but the workhorse.

"'Night," he said to George.

"See you in the morning."

Jack returned to the tent, but Lily said nothing as

he slipped inside. He found Nala on his bed again and began a wrestling match that ended in a draw, with him under his blankets and the big dog stretched out beside him, half under Lily's cot. The rest of the night involved Nala's steady encroachment onto his territory with the relentlessness of any claim jumper. Even sleeping on the deck of the steamer had been more restful than this.

Small wonder he did not hear Lily rise, but came awake to the sound of many male voices and Lily's clear soprano piping above the rest.

"Seconds are a nickel more."

Jack opened his eyes and glanced about the empty tent. The aroma of fresh-brewed coffee brought him to a sitting position and the mouthwatering fragrance of biscuits had him into his boots and out the tent flap.

There stood Lily behind a plank table which held a giant cast-iron griddle filled with fluffy brown biscuits. Beside that sat the coffeepot that looked as if it had been kicked down a long and rocky slope.

"Oh, there you are at last. Mind the table while I check the next batch. It's fifteen cents for black coffee and one biscuit. No seconds on the coffee."

With that she left him to the line of men holding empty cups and bandannas. Jack burned his fingers trying to lift out one of the golden cakes and there-after used the spatula. He'd only two left when she reappeared with a square bake tin filled with a new supply.

"I've never seen a more industrious individual in my life," he said.

She smiled at him and then went back to pouring coffee while he stayed staring after her. He'd never met a woman like her. She was a dynamo of activity. Had it been only yesterday he had judged her worthless as a partner? It was obvious now that Lily was more than she appeared.

Chapter Five

Jack noticed that some of the men brought her a half cup of coffee beans instead of cash, which she collected in a bag on the table. The coins went into a small can. Nala spent her time scouring the ground for any crumbs left by the hungry stampeders. When the second pan was empty she called to the men still waiting in line.

"That's the lot, gents."

A groan rose from the line, but they shuffled off.

Lily collected her pot, can and tins. "The board and crates go just there."

Jack disassembled the makeshift table and followed her inside where Lily divided the remaining dough and greased the pan. She cooked two lovely fat biscuits, offering Jack one. They drank the remains of the coffee black and strong.

Nala sat without begging, which surprised Jack.

"Doesn't she like biscuits?" he asked.

"I give her all she can eat, once a day."

"What about table scraps?"

She leveled him with a cool eye that made him pause to wonder what he had said to earn such a look.

"There aren't any." As if to prove her point, Lily used her index finger to retrieve all the crumbs from her plate. "I've got to go down to collect fares from the arriving ships and you can help me today. Tonight we'll buy whatever we don't have and set off tomorrow."

"What about my gear?"

"Did you meet George?"

Jack nodded.

"I'll pay him to watch the place. He'll be happy to have a job that requires only sitting and smoking."

They were down at the beach a few minutes later. It was a long day, helping men collect their goods and carrying them to the hotel. Lily used Jack like a second pack animal, but he didn't mind, because the labor kept him from dwelling on the past.

As they took the last man up the hill, Jack caught Lily staring speculatively at him.

"What?" he asked.

"Never expected you to last 'til noon."

It amused him that as he was judging her, she had been judging him and finding him lacking. Had he improved her opinion of dandies?

"Were you? It's hard not to judge on what you see," he said, thinking of himself more than her.

She nodded her agreement at that. "It's a rare man willing to do a full day's work. That's why most of them will fail. They're better at spending money than making it."

"Perhaps I'm the exception."

She grinned and nodded. "I hope so."

That evening they purchased the foodstuffs they needed and Lily collected her sled. The tent, clothing, snowshoes and food all fitted nicely. His tools and equipment did not. That left over seven hundred pounds. Lily tried several times to get him to leave the "uselessness" behind, but failing that, she rented a pushcart that he could use to the base of the Chilkoot. From there he would have to tote his belongings. Lily sold her tent and contents to George Suffern who had sold his lot to a new arrival, and all was ready for their departure.

Jack slept better the second night, his day's labors gracing him with a weariness that kept him from both restlessness and dreaming.

Nala woke Jack by stepping on his face and he sat up in time to see Lily's lovely pale shoulders disappear beneath her shirt. It was a sight he wouldn't mind seeing each morning. He whistled a tune and rolled his bedding.

"You're in a fine mood today," she said, turning

toward him as she fastened the last button and drew on her coat.

"Departure day," he said. "Just happy to be on our way."

She lifted her eyebrows as if she were not entirely convinced that this accounted for his gaiety. "They say a light heart makes for an easy journey."

The smile faded from his face. A light heart? His was still heavy with guilt and anger and confusion. Why had his father done it?

"What is it, Jack?"

He shook his head and gave her his back, packing up the last of his gear.

They ate cold biscuits and headed out before dawn, joining the others who set their feet upon the same trail.

Lily seemed in high spirits as she steered Nala through the mud, anxious to get out of town and onto the properly snow-covered ground so the sled would glide. But, though the ground was frozen, the march of many feet kept the ice from the trail. Lily worried aloud about the runners scraping over the rock, but there was nothing to be done about it. Five miles up they reached the first ford on the swift, shallow Dyea River. Lily refused to use the precarious jumble of driftwood and logs, not so much for the shoddy construction, but because the builder, named Finnegan, demanded a toll.

"We've been together three days and I've yet to see you spend a dime," said Jack.

"Nor will you until we reach the pass. We'll need all I've made when we get there and at the lakes for boat-building."

"That's true." Jack had exhausted most of his money on the journey and on his gear.

"I've been collecting coffee beans for months so I could sell coffee on the way. I figure the snow and the timber for fires if free." Lily looked uncertain now, hesitant. "Would you like me to help haul our gear across, or will I set a fire and sell coffee to passersby?"

He doubted she could sell much. Men were anxious to be on their way and still fresh from town, but he didn't say anything that might hurt her feelings. Plus, he thought she'd be more hindrance than help, so he set her off to the opposite side to set up her stand, leaving himself to the important work. He spent the next three hours towing their gear over, one load at a time.

Lily built a little fire and brewed coffee and cooked beans, which she sold for two bits a plate to the passing greenhorns, doing a brisk business. She brought him a portion and he ate it so fast he nearly choked.

"I didn't think I was hungry."

She retrieved her plate and patted his cheek before turning back to her fire. When he finished the last load, she scattered the burning logs and they ate what was left of the beans.

The trail up the opposite side of the creek was easy, with only a gentle slope. It did, however, reveal glimpses of the looming range they must breach to attain the interior.

Nala pulled the sled effortlessly, while Jack struggled with the cart as the wheels continually bogged in the soft spots on the trail.

"Someone should throw some gravel in this patch," he grumbled.

Lily laughed. "Are you going to stay behind and fix the road?"

He shook his head.

"Nor is any man, for it would only make it easier for the next. It's a race, don't you know?"

Jack realized she was correct. He was no longer in the theoretical world of textbooks and hypotheses. He was not about to build a model; everything hung on his ability to bring his materials to the gold and put his invention to use. Lily was right. The swiftest would have the best claims. There would be no prize for those who came too late. He knew his history and bore no illusions. The best ground would have been taken before news reached the outside, just like in California. Thank goodness his machine did not depend on his securing a virgin claim, for he did not plan to surface-mine, but instead to tunnel into the frozen earth. If it worked as he intended.

For a time he walked silently, carrying his hopes and doubts. The trail grew far worse, cutting through spruce, hemlock and cottonwood. The narrow path became a tangle of roots, laid bare as skeletal arms by the army of marching feet.

They reached a stretch where Nala could not pull the sled and Jack's cart became more a hindrance than a help.

So he called a halt. "This is the easy part of the trail?"

Lily said nothing to this, her breath coming in streams of condensation in the cold air.

"We have to portage this part," he reasoned.

She nodded.

He made the first trip carrying what he estimated to be over a hundred pounds. Nala carried loads of thirty. They inched along, cutting back, retrieving goods, carrying them only as far as they could see the trail. And all the while men streamed past them, making a similar relay. Lily was happy to reach the river once more, where the cart again rolled on the coarse gravel that wound around the enormous boulders.

Glaciers, he realized. Only a massive moving mountain of ice could have set such huge rocks here.

They crossed the river twice more before reaching Pleasant Camp at sunset. Jack's shirt was soaked with sweat and both he and Lily had wet feet. Even Nala groaned as she settled at her mistress's side.

The camp was only a grove of a few trees and moss perched on the rocky ground, giving them a place to throw a rope between two spruce trees and hang a bit of canvas. Lily gathered wood and began a fire as Jack reordered their gear.

"Only seven miles today," Jack said glumly, thinking of the four hundred and ninety-three remaining as he came to sit beside the fire. "I'd hoped to reach Sheep Camp today."

"And I'd hoped to find gold in this river and save ourselves the journey."

He stared at her, knowing that he could have made that camp if he'd had a male companion to help with the portages instead of doing the job of two men.

She set about soaking dried peaches as she mixed flour, salt and lard. When she rolled out the dough on a planed plank and set it on her cast-iron skillet he recognized what she was about. Sugar went into the rehydrated peaches, as well as cinnamon. The pie was covered with a second sheet and the dough trimmed and fluted. Finally she covered the skillet and buried it in a bed of coals. Jack's mouth watered at the aroma. Soon there were thirty men gathered, looking longingly at the skillet.

"Would your wife sell a piece of that pie?" asked one.

Jack was about to correct the man's assumption and send them off when Lily piped up.

"I'll be auctioning each piece. There's eight pieces

total." She eyed the gathering men. "Not enough for all, just like the gold in Dawson."

The greenhorns began jostling to get a look as Lily scraped the coals off the lid of the Dutch oven and peeked beneath. She shook her head.

"Not yet."

Jack realized that he would have none of the pie, and he was surprised at how much that disappointed him. He had prepared for hardship and deprivation. But his imagining had not included ignoring the scent of cinnamon and bubbling-hot peaches.

The first slice sold for $6 and the last for $14. Lily had made $76 on one large pie. As the auction winners returned their forks and plates, Jack began to resent that skillet, which he had to carry, but received no benefit from.

Their agreement included her feeding him, but he had not specified what the meal might be. He watched Lily soak a large dried salmon in a pot of water, then add oats and set the whole mess over the coals.

"Nala eats better than we do," he grumbled

"And she works harder than either of us," Lily countered, patting her dog. "Now stop sulking."

Lily took the fist-sized scraps she had trimmed from the pie and pressed them into a rough circle then added a cup of peaches she had set aside. She folded the circle into a crescent and placed the covered skillet back on the coals to cook.

"How much will that go for?" he asked.

"I'm not sure. Would you rather I sell your half, partner?"

He met her gaze and found her eyes twinkling. They shared a smile.

Lily shook her head in mock admonishment. "Men are all alike."

"I just wanted a bite."

She reached out and stroked his hand. "And you shall have it and half the money from the pie, or we can pool it for supplies."

Before he could stop himself, he had grasped her fingers. She was not quick enough to escape him. The tingling awareness flared again. He leaned forward.

"They thought you were my wife," he said, finding his voice low and gruff.

"Let them. It will keep them from all manner of foolishness on the trail." She glanced at her hand, still captured by his, and then at her skillet. "The turnover will burn."

Jack didn't care. He wanted to pull her into his lap, bend her over his arm and kiss those red lips. He leaned forward.

"Jack. Let go."

He did and she went about as if nothing had happened. But her cheeks flushed and her nostrils flared as they had when they had climbed that final slope. So, the brief encounter rattled her, as well. It was both disquieting and satisfying to know that he was not alone in his kindling desire.

She lifted the turnover and carefully flipped it, then replaced the lid and coal topping. A few minutes later Jack was juggling the hot, flaky pastry, trying not to let the thick, bubbly liquid escape to the ground.

He took a bite and burned his tongue. The icy water from the stream kept him from serious harm.

"Patience," she cautioned, blowing on hers.

He stared at the sight of her, lips pursed as she exhaled and felt the desire rising in him like the boreal tide off the Taiya Inlet. And now, staring at her, patience was the very last thing on his mind.

Just watching her made his insides bubble in molten energy, like the filling he gripped in his two hands. The urge to kiss her was irresistible. Damn, he wanted her more than he wanted the pie.

"You're beautiful," he said.

She laughed. "No, but I could be."

He didn't think it polite to disagree, but Lily was lovely as a cherry blossom, pink and fresh and sweet. "What do you mean—could be?"

"In Dawson, where the women are scarce, I figure, the fewer there are, the better I'll look."

Her giggle captivated him. He stared at her, really looking, and he knew she would be beautiful anywhere in the world, but somehow she looked most alluring by firelight under a starry sky. This wilderness suited Lily, her mirth making her cheeks rosy and her eyes sparkle.

Lily finished her half of the turnover and scoured her skillet with sand, then seasoned it with grease before packing it away.

He watched the easy grace of her movements and listened to her soft humming. Somehow Lily made him feel at peace. He wondered again about her and realized he knew next to nothing.

"Did you leave anyone back there, Lily?"

She turned and peered at him.

"Family you mean? Sure, plenty. I've got three sisters. And four brothers. I'm the oldest." Lily lifted her hand to start counting her siblings from bottom to top. "Cory is next oldest and working on the docks, then Bridget, employed as a kitchen maid in a fine house on the hill. Tried to talk her into coming. She's pretty and has a passable voice, but she has a sweetheart who shovels coal on a steamer in the bay and so she'd not have it. Mary is a fine seamstress. One day she'll have a shop if I've anything to say about it. Grace is working in the same factory. She's been at it since she was fourteen. Patrick and Joseph are a year apart, but you'd never know it. Linked at the elbow, those two, and hit hard times. They're out of work and taking what comes. My sisters are looking after them and will see they don't starve. Donald is the next. Bridget's lost track of him. He was heading south for work but they haven't a word."

She barely paused to draw breath. Her crates repacked, Lily joined him at the fire.

"What about you, Jack?"

"A sister, Cassandra, and my mother. That's all."

"Your father?" she asked.

"Gone." He stared at her wide blue eyes and felt a pang of guilt at the half-truth. "Yours?"

Lily looked away. "Oh, yes, he's gone, too. I don't remember him." Her voice sounded funny, strained, tight. She stood and gave him her back. Something was definitely wrong.

"Lily?"

"Shall we put the bedrolls here or there?"

"Are you all right?"

When she turned back her face was composed and she had that businesslike manner about her. "Of course."

But she wasn't, he felt it.

He wanted to ask her again, but it was obvious that Lily was doing her best to put the matter aside. He let her, for now. After all, he had secrets of his own to protect.

He set out their bedrolls.

Jack lay down and waited for her to do the same as he considered bringing her next to him in the night. Lily squashed that plan by calling Nala to lie between them, forming a living wall. Jack smiled. The hound and he were already good friends and he did not fear losing an arm. He petted the dog to test his certainty. The dog closed her eyes to savor his touch. Lily frowned.

Jack grinned. “Nala seems to like it.”

Lily narrowed her eyes, but said nothing to this as she turned from him, lying on her side and giving him her back.

Chapter Six

The following day they traveled the four gentle miles from Pleasant Camp to Sheep Camp, which they reached as the morning was only half spent. Jack had to give credit to Lily for she was a tireless worker. Despite her inexperience on the trail and inability to carry much weight, the woman had sand.

His spirits flagged as they struggled up Long Hill, shuttling their belongings a few hundred feet and then returning for more cargo. This way, Nala could make the trips with them, taking some of the load from Jack. They had sent the cart back early, for the trail was too steep and rocky to use it. Until they reached Lake Bennett, Jack would have to carry and pull like a mule.

To bolster his determination, he thought of his little sister, Cassie. When he made his fortune, he'd see she attended Wells or Vassar so that she had more than her good looks and a sizable dowry to recommend her as a wife—she'd have a fine education as well. His father had not thought it important that Cassie attend anything past finishing school, but Jack disagreed. Perhaps he would never finish his degree, but his sister would have a chance to finish hers.

Jack lifted another load, biting down with grim determination, as if he could see her there at the university. Yes, he'd get her there if he was damned trying.

Cassie's care was the job his father should have shouldered. But he was gone and so it fell to him. Jack lifted another crate full of tools and trudged along. Raising a refined, well-educated young lady, took money, lots of it.

Jack dropped the load beside the others. Lily had said she would carry only her gear, but she relented when she recognized he would not leave his "folderol" behind. She passed him with the empty sled, whizzing over the snow in the running tracks she had made, skirting around the line of lumbering men as she went.

Yard by yard they crept along the ground, like ants carrying a caterpillar, until they breeched the final hill and saw the last piece of flat ground from here to Stone Crib. Lily waited at the crest of the rise, motionless in the twilight as she stared out. He could see nothing but the men before him until he was nearly even with her and then he understood what had stopped them.

The little depression was filled to bursting with men and tents and gear. A center artery of traffic marched through the middle of the group. Beyond stood the Golden Stairs.

"Is that black line the trail?" asked Lily, her voice low and reverent.

"No, or not only the trail. Those are men, fixed in lockstep from bottom to top."

Her eyes widened at that.

"It's the Chilkoot Pass, the most devilish climb from here to hell and back. It rises a thousand feet in a half mile."

Lily continued to stare. "So that's it. My friend, Diinaan, told me that if you move from the trail to rest, you're hours getting back in line."

"Come on, let's get down before it's full dark."

The final three hundred yards took all Jack had. They set their canvas on the bare snow and Jack realized only belatedly that he had toted no firewood from Sheep Camp. He fell back into his blankets exhausted and began to doze.

Lily prodded him awake.

"What am I to cook on?"

Jack did not open his eyes. "I'm not hungry."

She sniffed. "Perhaps not, but Nala is and the food is frozen."

Jack sat up. Nala had to eat. He looked about at the fires of other camps. Lily stared down at him with eyes flashing fury. He'd not seen this look before. Her tight expression radiated discontent and he found he didn't like disappointing Lily.

"Isn't that just like a man to set off with no plan at all?"

"I'll get some," he said, already on his feet but she marched over to the closest fire and set into conversation with the stampeders gathered there.

After a few minutes she returned for her kettle and Nala's food. Jack roused himself to set the camp properly and when he had finished organizing their gear, she returned with the kettle nearly full of oats, rice and two large strips of reinvigorated dried salmon.

His mouth watered as she set the offering before Nala, who ate every single morsel and licked each stray oat from the kettle.

"I agreed to make them cornmeal biscuits," Lily informed him.

"We don't have cornmeal," Jack pointed out.

"They do. In return we'll have two strips of bacon each along with three biscuits, plus use of their fire to make our own coffee."

The woman negotiated everything and always seemed to come out ahead. Jack joined the men to watch Lily melt snow in her skillet, to which she added bacon grease and cornmeal until she had a fine dough. The aroma of biscuits cooking with the bacon drew many longing looks from weary men. Jack thought some gathered just to look at Lily.

"You'd make a fine cook in Dawson, ma'am," said the rangy one, whose name Jack could not recall. It hardly seemed useful to remember names.

"If the money's right, but I'm thinking I'll do better singing in the bars," she said, giving them a smile that stunned them speechless.

The man with the deeply lined face asked her for a sample. Lily grinned at her audience and began to sing as she tended the biscuits.

The men shut their eyes to savor her sweet voice. Yes, Lily would do well, very well, if they survived the trip. Jack felt the weight of responsibility pressing on his weary shoulders.

When she'd finished they shared what they knew of the trail. The man who they called Cincinnati leaned in, conspiratorially.

"I got it from a grave digger from Baltimore that the Mounties are at the top of that." Cincinnati motioned to the trail, shrouded in darkness but still looming before them all.

"I should think that would keep order," said the rangy one.

"That ain't all. He was turned back because he didn't have the one ton of gear they're requiring to pass."

"What?" Lily's eyes widened in disbelief. "Why?"

"And they're checking food supplies. If you ain't got a year's worth of grub, back you go."

Jack and Lily exchanged a long look.

"It's to keep men from getting up in those mountains and starving to death, I'm sure," said Jack. "It's sensible."

"Well, *we'll* not be turned back," said Lily.

Jack was growing to like that stubborn set of her chin and the fire in her eyes. The gal was full of piss and vinegar and he was starting to believe that having her as a partner might not be the worst he could do.

"How you planning on getting that grub?" asked Cincinnati.

"You said the grave digger turned back, didn't you?" asked Lily.

He nodded. "After his first trip up them Golden Stairs."

"Then others will, as well, and they won't want to haul their gear all the way home, will they?"

And damned if she wasn't right. As he set about the labors of carrying his gear to the summit one painful load at a time, Lily inventoried what they had and assembled what they lacked, a collection that nearly mirrored the list the Mounties recommended, including 150 pounds of bacon, 75 pounds of raisins and 400 pounds of flour. Then she paid a Chilkat Indian hauler to carry everything to the top, where she waited, just past the checkpoint, guarding their belongings as Jack made trip after trip with his gear.

It took Jack ten days to finish the last climb up the fifteen hundred steps cut into the ice and snow, wearily dragging himself along the guide rope with the rest of the stampeders. The line of men groaned and sighed, heaved and swore up the thirty-degree incline. Many turned back and each one that did gave Jack more determination to be among the ones to reach Dawson.

"That's the last of it," he said, sinking beside Lily on her canvas tarp. "I'd have been here sooner if I had a partner who could carry."

"If you had a partner who could carry, he'd have been dragging his own gear up the pass, not yours. I saw my gear delivered and without you lifting a finger, plus the food stores those redcoats required."

Jack looked at her gear which had returned to its original size, meaning that she no longer carried the food. "Where is it?"

"Jack, you can barely manage your working model and I don't want to overload the sled. I sold most of the food."

"Did it occur to you that you might need it at Lake Bennett?"

"It did, but money is easier to carry."

"Supplies will be more dear."

"In as short supply as women, I wouldn't wonder. Imagine all those clothes falling to ruin and all those hungry men, desperate for a hot meal and a bit of entertainment."

"You should have asked me."

She handed him a biscuit and coffee. "Yes, I should have."

Her contrition and the food melted his ill-humor.

Lily narrowed her eyes on him. "Do you want your half of the money now or at Lake Bennett?"

Jack disliked handling money. "You keep it for now."

She tilted her head. "You sure?"

He nodded and Lily shrugged, setting about the process of making their supper. After a while she handed him a plate.

Jack accepted it gratefully. He'd not had to cook a thing since he'd hit the beach. It made him feel guilty for his temper over the food supplies.

"I'm sorry I was short with you, Lily. The money's yours, not mine."

"Some of it maybe. But some I earned since we were together. That means you get a say in how we spend it."

He took a forkful of beans, chewed and swallowed, then nodded. He helped her clean the plates with snow and packed the kitchen box. She gave him a wary look at first, but allowed him to do as he liked. After supper they settled with their coffee by the fire, Lily with an arm around Nala and Jack on her other side. Lily no longer used her dog as a wall between them, allowing Jack closer at meals. He liked her company. She didn't talk drivel, but kept them on practical matters. Every so often she spoke of her plans. He liked that best, for she looked off at the horizon when she spoke, her body finally still, her hands at rest and her face holding a look of such longing, it about did him in. He admired her dreams and her drive.

They set the tent and Jack loaded his stove with wood to keep them warm at night. The next day they began the descent to Crater Lake. The trail was difficult but at least downhill. It was unfathomable that the distance between the Scales, below the Chilkoot Pass, and Crater Lake was less than five miles. They were well and truly into the mountains now. The wind bit deeper and the snow fell faster. They used Lily's sled for all the gear, making short trips and shuttling forward, bit by bit. Jack worried every step that they would not reach Lake Bennett in time to make a proper shelter before the real cold hit. It was November already and still they had not reached that last great lake. The nights were twenty hours long now, so they traveled by moonlight and by the shimmering Northern Lights. When they stopped they huddled together, the three of them, dog, man and woman, in their blankets by the fire, and still he never felt warm.

When the cold grew so deep that the coffee froze in his cup before he could drink it, Lily finally convinced him to cache some of his gear so they could move forward. And still it was January before they reached Bennett. This would be the launching point for the boats, because it was the first of the connected lakes that became the Yukon River.

As they descended the final incline, the narrow lake seemed only a bare expanse among the trees, surrounded by an odd assortment of structures, hastily erected and shoddily made. Lily signed on to help a woman run her kitchen, which did a better business feeding men than any other in the vicinity. Instead of pay, she received food and shelter for them both. That freed Jack from having to build a cabin, so he had time to retrieve the remainder of his gear, using Nala and Lily's sled. On each return trip he found more and more men building their boats on the shore so as to be ready for the break-up when they would sail to Dawson. When, at last he had all his belongings, he turned his attention to constructing their boat.

Jack planned their conveyance carefully, since it had to carry more weight than most. It needed a reinforced hull, which would make it heavy and unwieldy. He took the problem to Lily. She did not understand construction but he trusted her opinion.

"I'm afraid I won't be able to see past the gear piled in the middle."

"Make it longer, then the gear won't go as high."

"I've made it the length of the pines here. It will be sturdier that way."

She nodded at the logic of that and then considered his drawing, pointing to a spot in the bow. "If I stood here, I could see for you."

"You'd spot for snags and rocks." He nodded, liking the idea, for it kept him from having to construct a raised steering deck and extending and weakening the rudder. "Yes. That might work."

They shared a smile, which Lily ended when Jack tried to stroke her cheek.

"Off to work with you. You can't build a boat while standing in my kitchen."

He spent the next hour looking through his gear for his whipsaw and tools, finally returning to Lily.

"I think they've been stolen."

"Don't be silly, I'm a better watchdog than all that." She paused, coffeepot in hand on her way past a long table of seated men. "I rented the saw to George Murphy and his brother, Tim. Larry Kristen has your hammer, but no nails. Those he has to buy elsewhere. Martin—"

"You *rented* my tools?"

"Well, you didn't need them to haul freight. Now that you're back, I'll only rent them at night, or would you prefer to work nights? I can get more for them in the day." Lily must have read the answer in his darkening expression for she lifted a hand. "Days then. The sun is only up for two hours a day." Jack grumbled. "I'll see you have them all tomorrow, first thing."

She headed toward the kitchen and he stormed behind her, frustration boiling over. Why must he stand in line to use his own tools?

"You had no right to rent what is mine."

That stopped her in her tracks. She thumped down the heavy pot on the sideboard and pressed her fists deep into the folds of her skirt.

"And whose dog and sled are you using?"

Jack ground his teeth together at her point. The fact that her point made perfect sense only annoyed him further.

"Lily, you said we're partners and we share what's ours."

She nodded, but her expression remained uncertain. "That's so. You shared my sled. I shared your tools."

Jack scowled, finding no ready answer to this and wondering why her logic made him even madder than before.

"We've a need for money to buy the fittings and hardware for the boat," she said.

That was also true, and he should have accepted her reasoning, but he found it did nothing to assuage his annoyance. It seemed he couldn't be near her at all lately without picking a fight and most of those fights made no earthly sense afterward.

And then it struck him. He wasn't here about the

tools or hardware. His heart was not pumping and his skin was not flushed out of ire. He came back again and again to fight, because this was as close as he could come to satisfying the emotions she stirred in him. He was here looking for a fight when what he really wanted, what he really needed was—Lily.

He took her by the shoulders. Her mouth dropped open in surprise as she recognized what he was about to do an instant too late. This time he wouldn't let her slip away. This time he'd have what he came for.

Jack drew her in, slanting his mouth across hers, taking possession of her. She stiffened at the contact and then threw her arms about his neck, pressing her body tight to his.

Finally, Lily was in his arms.

Chapter Seven

Her fingers tugged in Jack's hair, demanding more as he met her soft lips. The desire he had smothered each day and every night now roared within him. He pressed down hard, feeling the heavenly softness of her lips crushed against his. He opened his mouth, silently demanding she do the same. Her lips parted and he thrust inside, savoring her wanton little moan and the slick, silken texture of her mouth. Her tongue danced with his as he cradled her against his body, pressing her back. At last, he supported her weight and still she clung to him with all the fierceness of a tigress. He'd known she would be just this way and the proof fired his blood and aroused his fantasies. Lily's surrender held the sweetness of honey and the heat of a branding iron. No matter how closely he held her it was not enough.

Somehow, he had surmounted her barricades and he basked in the delight of her soft body, full breasts and thrilling little cries of excitement. He laid her across his arm, wishing he were alone so he could take off her top and cup her lovely full breasts in his hands. How many times had he imagined holding her like this— And here was a battle he could win, a battle that made sense, perfect sense.

She'd let him. Her kiss left no doubt. He could do all the things he'd imagined as he lay beside her night after night on the frozen ground. He'd never wanted anything so much as he wanted Lily. Why hadn't he done this weeks ago instead of bickering about this or that?

Lily's hands were tugging at his shirttails. A moment later she had them up and out of his trousers, her fingernails raking over his skin, arousing him to madness. He eyed the table behind them and draped her half across it.

A pot clattered to the floor and Lily startled, then stiffened in his arms. An instant later she turned her head away, depriving him of her full mouth as she pushed against his shoulders.

"Let me up, Jack."

Somehow he'd taken her to the table beside the kitchen stove, where her employer, Sasha Cowdan, now stood staring at the two of them tangled together like newlyweds.

Lily slipped from his arms and tugged at her

blouse, her face flaming with embarrassment. Jack tucked in his shirt.

What the devil had gotten into him? He'd just wanted to speak to her about his tools. No. If he were honest, he'd admit he'd come for this, had wanted it since that day in her tent when she'd stroked his bare chest. And he would keep coming back for this as long as she'd let him. Lily was like a hunger now, something he could not control with his mind. He needed her body, her mouth, her throat.

And she needed him, too. Her kiss told him that. No wonder she'd held him off all these days and weeks. It wasn't to protect herself from his unwelcome advances. It was to keep him from learning they *were* wanted.

"I'm sorry," she said to Sasha.

He wasn't. He'd never be sorry for something that perfect. Why hadn't Nancy ever kissed him like that? Why hadn't she held him as if she were drowning and only he could save her?

Lily elbowed him and then cast her gaze from him to Sasha. Jack had forgotten the woman was there again. He couldn't seem to see anyone or anything but Lily.

She glanced at Sasha. "He's sorry, too."

But he wasn't. He'd do it again when he had the chance, was already planning their next encounter. Somewhere private—their boat! Yes, he'd have her alone then under the stars with the northern skies glowing with their shimmering light.

"Jack. I don't know what got into you," said Lily, trying and failing in pulling off the rebuke.

Into us, he wanted to say, but he couldn't seem to speak as he stared into her blue eyes. Her lips were swollen. His mouth twitched in a satisfied smile. He'd done that to her. His kisses made her cheeks and neck flush a tempting pink and her lips full with wanting.

She placed a hand on her bodice, which was rising and falling in a manner that made him take another step toward her.

But she turned away, helping Sasha mop up the hot water which now steamed from the floorboards.

"Out of my kitchen, Jack Snow," said Sasha.

"Tools," he said to Lily.

"Tomorrow," she said without looking up.

"You'll bring them?" he asked.

She hesitated, biting her lower lip between sharp white teeth. How he wanted those strong teeth to score his skin as she raked her nails over his back again.

He waited, taking in the worry in her eyes. She *should* be worried, very worried. She had been wise to hold him off, had somehow succeeded. But now he knew her secret.

She wanted him, too.

"Well?" he asked.

"Yes, yes. Now go."

His smile held the sweetness of victory. She could come to him and he'd be waiting for Lily to forget her resistance and again give him the sweetness of her kiss.

He left them, wondering why he had ever thought he wanted a sweet, compliant woman when he could have wildfire. As he walked out into the night to cool his skin, he compared her to every woman he'd ever met and found each one lacking. Lily, despite her best efforts, had roused him to near madness with just a kiss. Why were all the women back there as pale and meaningless as their poorly painted watercolors and self-indulgent poetry? Not one could do a blessed thing except order servants about and primp. None of them could have walked all the way from Dyea.

He scowled up at the sky, wondering what it would feel like, for once in his life, to take what he wanted instead of doing what was expected of him?

Lily rose even earlier than was her custom to track down Jack's tools. She hoped to have them gathered and returned to his boat before he even rose from his bed on the opposite side of the large dining room.

Nala stood when Lily left her bedding and stretched, nose down, back arched and then shook as her mistress rolled her thin pallet and blankets. Her hound walked silently behind her as she slipped out into the dark predawn. The sun had begun to rise again, peeking up above the mountains with a dim, joyless light that never seemed to penetrate the clouds before falling back below the horizon for eighteen hours at a stretch. Lily covered her face against the cold and slid her hands out of her gloves so she could maneuver her sled behind the dog. She hung the lantern first and then gathered the leather straps.

Her dog stood still as Lily strapped her into her harness and then mounted the sled. Nala began to yip and bark in excitement as she bounced straight up and down in her harness traces waiting for Lily to draw on her gloves. The instant she had her feet secure upon the boards and gripped the drive bow, Nala was off, bounding on the fresh snow and breaking a trail with her massive chest. Lily laughed in delight as the wind burned her cheeks. The cold made her eyeballs ache, but she didn't care. She loved the thrill of dog-sledding. It seemed the perfect mix of exhilaration and beauty. In a few minutes they were away from the half-buried buildings and flying over the frozen lake. Here the wind had scoured much of the snow away, making it ideal for Nala to run with all she had. They traveled in a magic golden circle of light, provided by the lantern. The only sound was the slide of the runners as they scraped over the granular snow. Lily made a circuitous route to the camps of the men who used Jack's tools, stopping to gather them like fallen apples from the half-finished boats that lined the shore. The whipsaw was last and with that aboard she turned toward home. Nala now settled into a tireless trot that Lily knew she could maintain for hours.

As she left the lake, and slipped between the tall silent sentinels of trees, Lily marveled at how the snow crystals shimmered on the dark trunks of the evergreens and how the snow-laden branches dipped to brush the ground. She spied Jack's building site and smiled. When he rose the tools would be here waiting and best of all, she would not have to face him. For the only thing more exhilarating than riding her empty sled was kissing Jack Snow.

Something moved beside the boat. Lily pulled on the brake and called for Nala to halt. A man stepped into the circle of light. Jack, she realized.

Her heartbeat tripled as she stared at him, tall and handsome. He placed a gloved hand on the upturned boat and brushed off the snow.

Lily lowered her muffler and tried to speak, but her voice was breathless, as if she had been pulling the sled.

"You're up early."

His grin was charming, but the twinkle in his eye spoke of mischief.

"Following you."

"I have your tools."

Jack unloaded them. "Ride me back for breakfast?"

She hesitated. To say no would be rude, for he'd have to wade through the snow to return to the hotel. But to say yes was to allow him to stand behind her on the foot boards, his big body pressed close behind hers.

She didn't remember nodding yes, but a moment later he was there, encircling her, his arms reaching around her to grip the drive bow. She lifted the reins and Nala glanced back.

"Ya!" said Lily and they were off.

Jack laughed, echoing her excitement in the joyful sound. After a moment she steered them away from the hotel and out onto the lake, wanting Jack to feel the thrill of riding with Nala running full-tilt.

Her dog hit the lake at a run and they whizzed along, Jack gripping the bow as she leaned back against him.

He called her name and she turned her head, tilting it back to look at him as they raced over the frozen lake. But he didn't speak again, only moved forward to kiss her.

His mouth was hot and cold all at once and his tongue slipped along her mouth. She felt a moment's resistance, but she could not hold on. The world was flying by too fast and Jack was holding on too tight. Lily surrendered to the thrill of the ride and the kiss and the man who had found her weakness in him.

In a moment he broke free and howled like a wolf

to the dark sky. Lily laughed and turned them back for home. Nala slowed to a trot as they hit the deeper snow and brought them safely to the hotel.

"I'll never forget that ride if I live to be a hundred," said Jack.

Lily smiled, wondering if her mother would be proud of her. Was this the adventure her mother had intended? Had she known what would happen by releasing Lily into the world? It was such a marvel, this territory, and she now felt it flowing in her blood, becoming a part of her.

Jack stepped down and then turned to kiss her again. But Lily was ready this time.

"Ya!" she said, sliding away from him as Nala trotted toward the kitchen, where Lily stored her sled.

"You can't run forever," he called.

Perhaps not, she thought. But she sure could try.

Over the next several weeks Lily avoided him when possible as he worked tirelessly on their flat-bottomed boat. She had a knack for visiting only when the lakeshore was filled with other builders and by being on the far side of the room when they lay down to sleep.

He cautioned himself to patience. The break-up was coming—not just for the lakes, but for them, and with it, his opportunity to have Lily alone.

He built his craft on the shore, electing not to set it up on the ice as many others did for he feared the break-up's power and unpredictability. No one could say exactly when the ice in Lake Bennett would fail, but Jack expected it would be awe-inspiring. When he could not work for exhaustion, he gathered with other men to share what they knew of the river. He borrowed a tattered copy of the December fifteenth edition of the *Dawson City News,* now four months old. Jack had read the passage concerning White Horse Rapids often and knew it by heart.

> The rapids are a half mile long and dangerous. A reef of rock juts from the left shore as the river narrows and the water boils with waves running five feet in height. Here a long boat comes in handy as a short one falls mercy to the waves. The landing is to the left beyond the reef and to the right lie the graves of those who drowned in their attempt.

He had not shown Lily the article, for he saw no need to have a hysterical woman on his hands, but he did bring her to see his completed boat. She surveyed his work with a critical eye.

"You've doubled the planking on the bottom," she noted.

"To strengthen the hull," he said, noticing how her dark hair shone in the light.

"Then why not the front?"

"It's called the bow."

He tried for her hand and she stepped around the boat on the pretence of inspecting his handiwork, but actually putting the hull between them. He smiled. *Run, but you can't hide.*

"That's the part that's likely to hit the rocks at White Horse Pass."

He scowled, staring at the boat again, thinking that she might be right. "How do you know about the pass?"

"Did you think that because I'm Irish I can't read?"

He had indeed thought that. "Of course not."

She sniffed. "Men are laying wagers on the break-up. Odds say it will be on May twenty-fifth."

"Did you lay a bet?"

She laughed. "Jack, I don't lay bets, though I have occasionally taken them."

She glanced across the frozen lake. "Snow's already gone from the hillsides, but this ice is as stubborn as any Irishman, overstaying his welcome." She turned back to him. "I know it's May already, but do you think we'll see Dawson by June?"

"Possibly. July definitely."

"And the snows coming again by September. That's not long to lay your claim on the Eldorado."

"I won't be digging by a stream. Those claims will be long gone."

She sighed, the worry returning to her eyes. How he wished he could hold her and assure her that everything would be all right. But her concern was well justified. He'd been so focused on the possibility of being alone with her that he'd nearly forgotten the danger of the rest of the journey. Arriving late to Dawson would be the least of his worries.

"I hope you know what you're doing."

"Afraid you'll have to feed me all next winter, too?" He tried for a smile and failed. He wanted her so badly he ached. Did she have any idea how much?

Her composure slipped. "I promised you that I would help you all I can, Jack, and so I will."

"Lily?" He reached for her but she held up a hand to stop him.

"No, Jack. Not again. I know what you're wanting from me and now you know the way of it with me, as well. But I need you to understand. I made a promise to my ma to see more than the walls of our tenement. I'm here for an adventure and to be part of something bigger than myself. You've become very dear to me. But if you're thinking to have me, I'm asking you not to. I know a man like you doesn't choose a woman like me for long. I'm trying to be wiser than my ma. She fell to temptation a time or two. They didn't stay. Nor will you, Jack. So don't make me fall in love with you and then cast me off so you can return to New York alone."

"Lily, I never intended..." But he had intended exactly that. He'd had so little respect for his partner he was ready to do whatever she'd allow him to do and it shamed him. "You're right, Lily. You deserve better."

Lily stepped outside the restaurant to stare out at the frozen lake. It had been reported that the river beyond Bennett had already given way some eight days earlier and those with the smallest boats had dragged their crafts across the thinning ice in an act that Jack called lunacy. Perhaps, but they were already under way. Even so, she was still trapped. Stuck in this frozen purgatory between Dyea and Dawson and trapped between what she wanted and what she knew would come.

Taking Jack would be her ruination. She felt it in the marrow of her bones. Yet she wanted it so badly it pulsed inside her with each beat of her heart.

Soon the two of them would be sleeping together in a narrow boat. Lily feared what would happen then. For she did not think she still had the will to say no, and she didn't expect a man to have the will to deny his pleasure. Perhaps that was the way between man and woman, passion over common sense.

Why hadn't she chosen that little tailor for a partner instead of this big, handsome, unattainable man?

Jack had kept his distance since she'd asked him not to shame her. But the tension between them had not lessened. All that had changed was the new awkwardness they shared as they waited their release from the ice that trapped them here.

At first, the crack sounded like a rifle shot, but then it was followed by another and another. The ground under Lily's feet rumbled and one of the men shouted.

"The ice is breaking."

Lily dashed toward the lake with the others. She elbowed her way through the crowd. The lake seemed alive with slabs of ice pitching and colliding. They squeaked as they scraped across each other and exploded with sharp pops as the ice snapped under forces she could not imagine.

Lily's heart beat fast as the rumble started. Water surged through and around the thick platforms of ice, tossing them one upon the other. She scanned the shore, searching for Jack, needing to share this moment with him. She found him, eyes pinned on her as he pushed through the crowd.

"Look at it!" she called, her words lost in the rumble.

He looped his arm about her and drew her close as they turned to watch the bottleneck of ice gathering, piling upon itself over the roar.

"That won't last now that the water's flowing." His voice was a shout directly into her ear and yet she could barely make out his words.

She had not even finished nodding when the dam broke in the middle releasing a slurry of freezing water and ice down the center of the lake. Gray water foamed and frothed as it greedily snatched great slabs of ice and carried them along.

Men cheered, threw their hats and scrambled to load their boats. The break-up had come at last and the race was on again.

"Come on, Jack. We need to load the boat."

Chapter Eight

"Tomorrow," Jack declared as if he had some power of divination.

"Are you mad? We'll be the last to leave the shore and last into Dawson."

"I've counted over six thousand boats here. That and the ice will make a pretty picture. I'll not be taken down after coming this far and I won't put you on the river in this."

"But Jack—"

"Look." He pointed toward the water.

Lily took her eyes from the flowing ice to stare in the direction he indicated. There was a shabby little vessel no bigger than a bathtub.

"Do you want to watch that man drown or have to stop to fish him out of the lake?"

He had a point. Lily had been so busy working in the hotel that she had not had a chance to see much of the boat construction, though she did keep close tabs on Jack's progress.

He continued. "Plus those ice sheets could tear even a strong boat into pieces and pop holes in our hull like a child poking a finger through a paper wrapping."

Lily watched five men push a squarish boat, loaded high with gear, off the muddy bank and onto the tumble of ice now thrusting onto the shore. They heaved and strained as the weight of the thing bogged down. Then, in what seemed only a blink of the eye to Lily, the ice shifted, tumbling from beneath one of the men, casting him into the lake. His friend tried to grab him but he disappeared between the ice sheets. The men on shore shouted and danced but none ventured onto the unstable ice to try to find him. He came up again in the fast-moving slurry of ice and water. Men dashed along the shore and finally got a rope around him, but in the meantime the boat rolled, throwing all their gear into the lake.

Lily felt her stomach pitch as she pictured all they owned being lost to the bottom of Lake Bennett. She turned to Jack. He did not seem pleased to be proven right, but rather saddened by the confirmation as he sighed heavily.

"They're all mad," she said.

He stared out at the insanity unfolding before them.

"I've built a strong boat. But I don't know if

anything can withstand that." He motioned with his head toward the rushing water. "I'd never forgive myself if anything happened to you."

She nodded, suddenly in complete agreement. "We'll wait until you say so, Jack. I trust you."

On impulse she reached out to hug him, thankful that he was so wise amid the chaos. But then she recalled the last time she had held him and hesitated, drawing back to leave him standing with his arms open to accept her. He let them fall to his sides and a small line formed between his brows.

They stared at each other in awkward silence as the water crashed behind them. She couldn't warn him to stay clear of her and then throw herself back into his arms. It wasn't fair to either of them. But she yearned for the comfort and protection he could provide and longed to listen to her heart, as it whispered words of hope, instead of doing what was wise by keeping clear of him.

She'd seen the look of surprise on his face when she'd asked him to leave her alone if he planned to abandon her in Dawson. He'd confirmed her fears without so much as a word. He had planned to do exactly that. After all they had endured together, it hurt that she meant so little to him. Still, she should not be surprised. That was the way of the world. Lily was a realist. Men like Jack did not take up with girls like her, at least not in public and never for the long haul. Fate had thrown them together, and all she could do was try to prevent herself from becoming nothing more to him than some shameful little secret.

Funny that she thought her chances better with the heaving ice floes in the lake than in Jack's arms.

That afternoon Jack saw many more stampeders set off. In his mind he knew they should wait, but it was still hard to watch the others go. Huge floating blocks of ice bobbed along to the mouth of the lake where they piled up like rock candy on a stick. Jack loaded the boat and lashed everything down. He'd agreed to assist in the launching of other boats in exchange for similar help.

The following morning, Lily met him by the boat, which now rested the lakeshore. Her cheeks glowed rosily, for nothing enhanced her beauty more than being out of doors and on an adventure. She seemed made for this wild, beautiful country. He drew in the line and helped her aboard. Nala followed with a graceful bound and then set her large forepaws on the gunwales, her tongue lolling as she waited with Lily for Jack to climb aboard.

Yesterday, she'd told him that she trusted him. It was a precious thing and he knew it. He meant to be worthy of her confidence and to be certain his precious cargo reached Dawson safely. Only now the most precious thing aboard his eighteen-foot-long vessel was Lily.

He turned back to the boat, pushing off with the

help of two other men. Then they heaved the second vessel into the water. Jack's obligation complete, he waded out to his boat, climbed aboard and released the line. The current took them beyond him, the lake was alive with the skiffs, boats of balsa, barges, canoes, kayaks and one vessel that appeared to have been made of packing crates tied together with twine.

"That one looks like a coffin," Lily said, pointing to their right.

She sat fearless in his conveyance beside her mutt who sniffed the air as her ears and gums flapped in the breeze. What a novelty for the dog not to have to pull them along. The winds grew fierce at the northern end of the lake, dragging them sideways. Jack and Lily both leaned with all they had against the rudder, trying to hold them in the center of the lake.

"Glad I reinforced the thing with sheet metal," he shouted.

"You've a knack for building, Jack, and that's a fact."

He glowed at the praise of his partner.

His boat performed well, and by late afternoon they had reached the checkpoint at Marsh Lake where the Mounties confirmed that each person had 700 pounds of food.

"That man's crying," said Lily. She set her jaw and stared at the unfolding tragedy as one of the herd of stampeders was cut away from the rest.

"Hard to fail after coming this far," said Jack.

"He won't be the last." Lily's grim judgments, though accurate, were sometimes dispiriting.

Would they be among the few who completed the journey? They'd seen so many give up or be sent back. Jack swallowed back his uncertainty. He had no room for it.

The winds were good and his sail carried them across Marsh Lake, but he pulled in before they reached the mouth.

"There's still an hour left of light," she said.

"White Horse Rapids is next. We need more than an hour to get past that and we need full light. After that there's snags and sandbars and more rapids."

"You sound as if you've seen it."

"Only in my mind." But he planned to walk the cliff and see for himself. It was images of White Horse Rapids that had kept him up many nights, worrying. Tomorrow there would be more than risk, there would be danger. He wondered how the first of those who had set off had fared on the river. They'd faced the rapids with ice and water running as fast as it would at any time in the season. Tomorrow they'd take their turn.

"Jack, you're scowling like a man with a belly-ache. What's wrong?"

"Wondering if the boat will hold water on the White Horse."

"It will hold."

Did Lily have any idea of what was before them? He decided to explain it to her after supper. He turned the rudder and steered them up onto the muddy shore, where the mosquitoes waited to devour them. Lily started a fire and added damp wood to the logs. The smoke drove off the worst of the bloodsuckers, but the whine of their wings was persistent and maddening. As she worked, the temperature dropped and the flying menaces retreated.

Nala ceased snapping at the bugs and settled beside her mistress with a groan, as if she'd walked all the way across the lake. Other campfires sprang up along the banks. Few wanted to face the joining of river and lake in the dark.

Jack's back ached from manning the rudder and sails, but he said nothing of it as he sank onto a log. His attention turned from his sore muscles to dinner the moment he caught the aroma of the stew that Lily had apparently smuggled aboard, carrying the precious cargo all the way from the mouth of Lake Bennett without his even knowing. It was a welcome surprise and he rather enjoyed eating together from one pot. They sat side by side, dipping their spoons as they stared at the fire and beyond to the glint of ice floating past them.

His attention lifted to the ribbons of green and blue light that shimmered across the sky.

"Oh," she said, following the direction of his gaze. "The Northern Lights. So beautiful. It's one of the things I love best about the winter nights in the Yukon."

Jack looked up. The aurora borealis. The shimmering curtain of color was only visible on clear dark nights. They had seen them many times in Bennett, but this might be the last of them as winter turned to spring.

He smiled and drew her closer, keeping his arm about her shoulder as they gazed at the sky and was rewarded when Lily nestled against him. He drew a breath of complete contentment. Such moments of peace and splendor were rare on their journey.

"What else do you love?"

"Many things. The clear blue of the glacial ice and whizzing over the snow on the empty sled with Nala going full out and watching the mountain peaks at sunset when the colors change so fast you don't dare blink."

He prized those things as well, felt privileged to have experienced them with her. He didn't know when it had happened exactly, when he had fallen in love with this wild country. But he knew he'd miss it more than he ever imagined possible. The world here seemed so alive and vital and the people lived *full out,* as Lily had said. It was so different from the stale, stagnant world he had left. And to think, had he not come, he might never have known what he missed.

"I loved watching the break-up," he said at last.

"And leaning against the rudder beside you, eating your peach turnovers and listening to you barter." He sat contentedly beside his partner, feeling that this moment might be the most perfect of his life.

Lily drew a deep breath as she watched the lights shimmer and undulate across the wide sky.

"I think this is what she meant," she said at last.

"Who?"

"My mother. When she knew she was dying she waited until we were alone and then she told me to sell everything to the last tack and get out of there. She told me to fill my life with adventures so I didn't end up like her, dying with regrets for what she never did."

She lowered her head and Jack heard her sniff. He looped his other hand about her and hugged Lily. She buried her face in the lapel of his sheepskin coat for several moments. Jack held her, thinking of Lily beside her mother's bedside. If the woman hadn't told Lily to go, he would never have met her.

"You've done just as she asked," he whispered, his lips an inch from the top of her head. "Well, I'm glad to be a part of your adventures, Lily. Honored, in fact."

She drew back and wiped her eyes. "Do you think she'd approve?"

He nodded. "Most certainly."

He hadn't realized how sheltered he'd been in his private school and university, how little he had seen outside his own circles. It had caused troubles between them at first, but now he trusted her intuition and her opinion. He'd never felt that way with a woman before. But Lily was different in so many ways.

Like him, she didn't speak of her troubles, and, surely, hers were different than those of the privileged son of a successful business owner. But would she share them if he asked? He found himself needing to know her better. The last time he asked about her father she'd changed the subject. Should he try again? He decided his need to know her outweighed the risk that she might turn the tables on him.

"What does your father do?"

Lily's smile faded and she gave him a sharp look. "I don't know. He didn't stay around very long and I don't really remember him. Ma said he drank his wages mainly, and we were better off without him. But I know she missed him. I did, too, or I missed the idea of him." She shrugged, as if growing up without a father was of little consequence. But he knew better. It hurt to be abandoned, even if you were already a man when it happened.

He thought of his father and felt his mood darken as well.

He gave her a little hug and she gave a half smile, then patted his cheek. "What about you, Jack? Did you have a mother who kissed you good-night and a father who came home each evening to find his slippers and paper waiting?"

Her voice held a forced levity that tugged at his heart. Is that how she pictured his life? She wasn't far wrong, except it was all an illusion, the perfect couple and their lovely children, built on a shallow foundation that did not hold against the first flood. But he didn't let her steer the conversation away from her pain just yet.

"I'm sorry."

"Don't be. That's all said and done. And look at me now, here on a river that will carry us all the way to Dawson in your fine strong boat." Nala rolled against her leg and groaned, glancing at her mistress, who scratched her head absently. "And should I make my fortune there, I'll be able to help my family so they can see what a great, wide wonder the world is, as well. But I don't know if I'll go back myself. I'm starting to take to this territory. It seems a good place to me."

Jack didn't know why it troubled him that she should wish to stay, unless it was because he knew he had to go. He had obligations back there in the States, a mother and sister. With luck and hard work he'd make his fortune and then he could choose his own bride.

Jack glanced at Lily, knowing it was a lie, for he couldn't really choose any bride. There were rules to any game and he needed to abide by them if he were to gain reentry to that world. He couldn't, for instance, choose the daughter of an Irish immigrant without being shunned by one and all. It just wasn't done.

Jack lowered his chin and stared at the fire, smoldering with the glowing embers.

He understood the expectations and had abided by them his whole life, never feeling their constraint. He did now.

Lily still stared up at the rolling aurora dancing across the sky. Her profile was chiseled, with a pert, upturned nose and a sloping jaw that narrowed to her pointed chin. Her neck was stretched, revealing its long, lovely length. How he wanted to stroke it and feel her pulse race beneath his lips. She turned to him and smiled.

"What does *your* father think of your grand adventure, Jack? Good sport between college and a career?"

He was about to lie, as he would have done had anyone else asked a question that brushed so dangerously close to his family secrets. But this was Lily who had given him only honesty.

He braced himself and began with the truth. "I don't know what he would think. He'd be sad, I expect. Truth is, Lily, my father died before I left for the Yukon." He paused, wanting to tell her the rest of it, but years of practice at keeping up appearances stopped him again.

This half-truth grated. He wanted her to know what had happened because if he deceived everyone around him, even those closest to him, then how was he any different from his father?

She took his hand. He opened his eyes to find her staring at him with the sweetest look of sympathy upon her face.

"Well, that's a pity, Jack."

Pity—no that was something he did not need from Lily. He drew back into his protective armor, letting her see only what he was willing to reveal.

"Yes. It's why I came actually. I am his only son. He lost everything shortly before his death. So it fell to me to settle his estate. Nasty business, dealing with creditors, banks and lawyers. They left us quite destitute."

She raised her brow, but her face did not register shock or the look of distaste he'd seen so often among those he had counted as friends before his fall from grace. She didn't judge him and she didn't turn away in embarrassment. For Lily only saw whom he had become, not whom he had been. He squeezed her hand, happy he'd agreed to be her partner. Their meeting, which he'd originally counted as misfortune, had turned out to be lucky, indeed. He admitted to himself that she might just be the best thing that had ever happened to him. With her, he didn't feel sorry for himself or like the son of a failure in business. And he didn't think back nearly as often, for there was too much to look forward to.

"But you said you also have a sister?"

Jack smiled. "My little sister, Cassandra, and my mother are both staying with my mother's older sister, Aunt Laura. It has been very difficult for them, losing their home and all they ever knew. It was through no fault of theirs, you see."

"Bad things happen to good people all the time, Jack. Being good is no protection at all."

"I suppose. They are my responsibility now. They are both depending on me."

When he looked back at her, he found she gave him a steady assessing stare. What did she see?

"Now I understand why you didn't quit with the others, Jack. Your back's to the wall as well, isn't it?"

He nodded, wondering why he'd told Lily so much.

She took his hand. "Find your fortune then, for success is the best revenge."

Jack nodded at the wisdom of this. But he didn't want a fortune. He'd had that and now saw how it had insulated, softened and corrupted him. He was lucky for the chance to do something other than eat dinner at the club and attend social outings that he feared would now bore him silly. But then what else was there for him to do?

It was his job to pick up the pieces of the life shattered by the recklessness, inattention and shortsightedness of his father—wasn't it? He had thought so. Did think so. It was just that he was so far from them. It made it seem like some dream, instead of his reality—a life he barely recalled now. He looked about him at the dark trees silhouetted against the glimmering sky. Would all this become a dream as well?

He hoped not, because he wanted to remember each moment of this journey. He wanted to remember Lily standing at the bow of his boat, nose to the wind and hair flying out behind her.

Lily stifled a yawn.

Jack thought of his earlier plans to have her alone, to lure her to the boat and have his way with her. The impulsiveness and sheer recklessness of his thinking now embarrassed him. Lily was not a toy.

"Would you like to bed down here or in the boat?" he asked.

"Let's sleep in the boat, beneath a piece of canvas. It should keep most of the bugs off and block the wind," she said.

Lily had said let's, as in *let us.* Jack found he could not suppress the rush of heat that flooded him as his noble thoughts battled with his carnal desires.

"Cold will keep the bugs off and we'll be away before they're about." Did she notice the catch in his voice?

They stowed her pots and crawled back into the boat, lying on the flat wooden platform he'd hewn from logs. Nala jumped in and curled at their feet. Jack removed his boots and draped a piece of canvas across the gunwales. It was a far cry from the slim, fleet boat he used to row in the Delaware Canal at Princeton, but he was proud of his little vessel. It carried all their gear and still had ten solid inches above the water line. He prayed to God that would be enough.

It was the end of May now, he realized, and his classmates would have already graduated and would soon be setting about beginning promising futures. Jack found that his musings did not precipitate the familiar pangs of regret any longer. Time and distance made them seem less significant, or was it that he had prospects of his own?

Lily snuggled beneath the blankets beside him, the heat of her body warming him.

He pulled the canvas up, but she stopped him by placing a hand on his.

"Leave it back for a bit. I'd love to watch the lights."

He lay beside her, hands folded behind his head, staring up at the heavens at the miracle above them.

Lily settled her head on his chest, at the juncture of his shoulder and he curled his arm about her, determined to ignore the slow pulsing desire that beat with his heart.

"What's before us tomorrow, Jack?"

He admired that about her. She focused her energy

only on immediate obstacles. Should he tell her the truth?

"Don't be sugarcoating it for me. I can take it."

He chuckled, wondering what she'd do if he petted her head. He had spent much time thinking on what her hair would feel like. He rested his palm on her crown and she nestled closer allowing him to caress her hair. The rhythmic stroke and her gentle breathing calmed him.

"Marsh Lake is shallow. We may have to pole through parts and hope the winds don't ground us on a sandbar or snag us on logs."

"I'll watch ahead and spot for them," she promised.

"After that it's Big Windy Arm. Treacherous winds. Some say it's more dangerous than the rapids."

"White Horse?" she whispered, as if to say it aloud was to bring bad luck.

"Yes, and then Miles Canyon. The trick, I'm told, is to ride the hogback."

"What's that?"

"The ridge of white water coming together in the center of the rough water."

He felt her nod and continued.

"We try to ride it about half the distance, then swing right to avoid the rocks dead center. They look like spears, I'm told."

"Well, they'll be hard to miss seeing."

"And even harder to miss hitting as the water

rushes at them, then splits into two streams. They've got pilots for hire at the checkpoint."

"We'll not need one, Jack. You'll be pilot enough, I'm thinking."

"I've never shot rapids, Lily."

"And I've never been first mate, but we'll do it together as partners."

Jack didn't tell her that she'd not be along for either White Horse Rapids or Miles Canyon, for he meant to set her ashore to portage the rapids to keep her safe. If he was lucky and survived the passage, he'd pick her up below.

"What are you not telling me, Jack?"

Damn. How did she know him so well?

Chapter Nine

Jack woke to find Lily curled snug against him. Her breathing had left a fine dusting of frost on his coat, but her body had kept him warm. He'd never slept beside a woman like this, in quiet tenderness, and he liked it more than he had any right to. It was a joy he'd never expected.

A shout came from close by and he realized the voice came from the river. The sun had not even crested the trees and already the parade of boats had begun. He sat up and Lily groaned in protest.

He glanced about at the dark outline of boats gliding along. The lake was crowded with vessels already.

Lily took Nala ashore and Jack prepared to cast off. She didn't keep him waiting. He pushed off and hoisted the canvas wave catcher. He'd learned of the triangular sheet from his discussion with a man called Cap'n Hegg. This sail helped stabilize his vessel and kept the wind from dragging them across the lake. Next Lily raised the square center sail, which she had stitched with an awl as nimbly as any New England whaler. And they were off, wind whistling past him as he turned the rudder. His blood rushed with the water that pulsed beneath the hull.

"Look out, Jack," called Lily, pointing at a low-riding skiff that cut before them and seemed without rudder.

The skiff careened sideways. Jack pulled hard to the right, sending Nala thumping to her side and then scrambling to her feet with much clicking of toenails on the deck. Lily clutched the gunwales as the wind left their sails.

Jack swore as the boat shot before them, nearly brushing their side. The men on board had perhaps three inches of freeboard above the water line, and Jack thought they had no chance once they hit the chop farther out, for though Marsh Lake was shallow, the winds tossed the water into three-foot swells.

"Jack! Look."

He followed the direction of her gaze and saw two boats collide. The one struck broadside floundered and filled, sending the men out into the lake. It sank out from under the occupants so fast there was no time to save a thing. The men were hauled aboard the craft that had scuttled them, and the swearing carried over the water. All about them men fought the wind and the water, the worthiness of their crafts and each other.

The farther north they traveled the bigger were the ice floes. He had hoped the largest pieces would have cleared this portion of the water, but it was not so. As the sky brightened to a steel-gray, they moved along with the heavy, dangerous bludgeons. Jack's stomach churned as they struck one and then another. The dull thump vibrated through the beams below his feet, like rolling thunder. His hull was double-thick, but would that be enough?

Lily moved to the bow and leaned out. Jack wanted to call her back, but he realized that with the sail and the center load he could not see well enough to steer them clear.

"There's another. Right, Jack."

He turned them and was horrified to see a slab of ice the size of a riverboat bob past.

"Slight left," she called.

This was a large tree, roots sticking up six feet above the water's surface. Not having a line of sight proved more disconcerting than he'd imagined and he wondered if his need to carry his gear would jeopardize Lily's life. Nothing aboard was worth that. He gripped the rudder with sweaty hands and looked to Lily who charted their course. He'd need a man to do the job when he set Lily ashore.

"Lake's ending!" Lily pointed to the passage.

Jack leaned out to see the white water. Nala seemed to sense what was to come, because she dropped to all fours and sank to the bottom of the boat. Lily gave her a reassuring pat and then resumed her place at the front, clutching the gunwales and bracing.

Swift water was what he had been told, but that did not prepare him for the flume or the pulsing thrum of water rushing through the narrow channel. Before him the bow lifted and Lily was momentarily two feet above him. In the time it took his heart to beat, the boat rose and then fell, thumping the river that now seemed solid as stone.

They no longer needed the sail and it hindered his sight, but how to lower it now that they were speeding along? Lily left her place and crept aft, hand over hand, like a baby learning to walk. She was making her way to the mast.

"Go back," he called and then thought better of it. If they were hit by ice she'd tumble off into the river, but the bow was not safe, either. Jack could barely swallow past the dread over her safety for he knew he'd have no chance to rescue her before he shot past. "Get down!"

But she either could not hear him or would not listen for she continued. Jack clutched the rudder and braced, trying to hold their course to the center of the white water as Lily reached the mast. A moment later, the canvas flapped madly. She gathered the flaccid sail and had one side secured when they pitched to the left and she sprawled over the boxes, sliding off and onto the deck. He released the rudder to rescue her and the boat immediately turned sideways, tilting dangerously. He glimpsed the water and the catastrophe that loomed as he dove back for the rudder to bring them about.

"Stay there!" she shouted, pointing a finger at him as if he were her second hound.

Jack gritted his teeth and pulled, bringing them around. Lily regained her feet and managed to tie down the rest of the sail.

He could see more clearly now, though the blind spot directly before him was troublesome. He compensated by searching far ahead and steering accordingly. That was how he noticed the red flag tied to a pole on the left bank. Below it was a sign, black paint on a wood slab. It read: Cannon.

Did the writer mean *canyon?* Could they have journeyed twenty-three miles from Lake Marsh already? Jack thought back to the blur of water and rushing shore, feeling certain they *had* reached Miles Canyon, the stretch of rapids second only to White Horse. Already he heard the dull roar of water.

He grounded them. There was a portage here, but the half-mile of skids, a kind of wooden railroad track, complete with cart and mule team, would have many other vessels waiting before them and it would take several days before their turn. The rapids themselves would take no more than ten minutes to cross or to finish them entirely.

Lily stared at him. Confusion wrinkled her brow. "What are you doing? We've the rapids next."

"Not we," he said.

Lily gaped at him a moment and then her mouth snapped shut as her eyes narrowed. Jack braced for a different kind of rough water.

"If you're thinking of leaving me behind, I'll not have it."

"We have to stop at the checkpoint." Jack indicated the large tent beside the Canadian flag. Nala jumped overboard before they'd even grounded, but Lily did not leave the boat.

"I'll wait here," she said, then folded her arms and glared as if daring him to try to drag her out.

He didn't, but instead lined up with the others. The officer asked the man before him for the address of his next of kin. That gave Jack a momentary pause as he imagined his mother receiving a letter from the North-West Mounted Police and winced. But when it was his turn, he gave the address and in return received a serial number and instructions to paint it on both sides toward the bow.

"We've checkpoints along the way. Expedites searches for the missing." The Mountie held the pencil over the ledger and glanced up at Jack. "Any others aboard?" asked the Mountie.

He hesitated then said, "My partner."

"His name?"

Jack swallowed. "L. Shanahan."

"His next of kin?"

"None," said Jack, feeling the sweat pop out on his brow. Lying was one of the traits he hated, for hadn't his father's whole life been a lie? Yet he'd done it to keep Lily with him.

"Women and children are required to walk the rapids. Any others?"

Jack stared. "Just the dog."

The officer dismissed him with a nod.

The seriousness of what he was about to do struck home, by not listing Lily, he'd prevented her family from ever knowing what became of her, should something happen. Jack turned back to the Mountie.

"How many lost so far?" Jack asked.

"Ten the first day and fifty-six boats. Though at least twelve sank before they even reached the center of Lake Bennett. Lucky for them as they didn't drown. Safe passage." He turned to the man in line behind Jack. "Next."

Jack headed back to the boat in a daze, wondering what he would do if anything happened to Lily.

Lily straightened as she saw Jack's odd expression. Anxiety pushed away some of her anger. His pale face and haunted eyes did not bode well. What had he learned?

"Nothing good, I'll wager," she whispered and pulled Nala close to her side.

Jack laid it out for her. Women were not permitted to ride the rapids, but he'd listed her as L. Shanahan and had not listed her next of kin.

"Rather go missing than have them know I drowned," she said.

"You should walk," he said.

"So should you. Be better than trying to pilot the boat alone."

"I'll take on another passenger."

"Their gear will weigh you down and experienced pilots charge $200 per boat. I checked."

"It's worth the money not to lose the lot."

She pictured the boat capsizing and Jack spilling into the river. "If we spend it on a pilot, we'll have nothing when we get to Dawson. What will you do with all your gear and no claim?"

"We might not make it if we don't."

"I can swim. Can you?" She didn't mention that her swimming experience involved being thrown into the bay and nearly draining it dry before someone pulled her out.

He nodded. "But no one can swim in that."

Lily looked into Jack's eyes and saw the worry.

"Jack, I'll pay for a pilot if you say so. But I'll not leave you alone on that boat with a stranger."

"A pilot won't take a woman. And the wait is four days."

"Four! It's too long. We could be halfway to Dawson by then."

He held her gaze and she knew that they could also be buried at the side of the river in the same amount of time.

Some of the fight went out of her. "What do we do, Jack?"

"I designed the boat to the weight of our equipment, so I can't take on more gear. I need to find a spotter, but I don't want to risk your life, Lily."

"But I'm your partner, Jack. If you're going, then so am I."

"Don't ask me, Lily. I couldn't live with myself if something happened to you."

Lily clasped his hand and stepped close. "Then steer us safely through."

Jack gathered her into his arms and rested his chin upon the top of her head.

"I never imagined I'd grow so attached to you, Lily."

She smiled at this and drew back. "And I'd be hard-pressed to pick between you and Nala."

"I don't snore or shed," he offered and she laughed again.

The laughter died as she watched him paint the serial number on both sides of the hull. Then she climbed aboard and hid beneath the blankets as he recruited four men to push them off the bank. Once they were beyond the reach of the Mounties, Lily emerged to see the steep gray walls of Miles Canyon rising beside them, constricting the river to one-third its breadth. The water sloshed against the cliffs and spilled back into the white water.

"Beyond the curve lies a whirlpool," called Jack, his voice losing the battle with the increasing roar of the water.

Lily swallowed hard, but did not regret her decision. They were partners and they'd see it through together.

The canyon seemed to rush at them. Jack leaned on the rudder, sending them first right and then left, weaving through the waves that burst up against the hull, splashing Lily from one side and then the next and then both at once. The boat pitched down, then bobbed up, sending Nala into Lily and taking both their feet out from under them. They rolled about, unable to gain their footing as water poured in over the sides. Above them, the gray menacing cliffs closed in.

Lily dragged herself up as they burst from the limits of the canyon to the rocky bank beyond. Freed from the constriction of solid vertical rock, the water swept out, filling the space. And then she saw it, dead ahead.

"Whirlpool!" she shouted and pointed to the right, looking back to see Jack staring at her, but he did not change course.

He couldn't see it, nor could he hear her. She motioned madly to the left.

Jack swung the rudder right, sending them careening away, but the boat now leaned dangerously, the load making them top-heavy on the sharp turn. The portside gunwales dipped and water spilled into the boat.

Jack stared in horror, first at the whirlpool, then at his listing boat as ice water poured into the hull. He straightened the rudder, heaving against the force of water and held as the whirlpool skittered them sideways. The boat righted with six inches of water sloshing in the bottom. It would stay afloat, he was certain.

His frantic heartbeat marked the seconds the whirlpool held them and then with a swiftness that seemed impossible they were cast back into calm waters and wide even banks. They had navigated their first rapids, but they had come within a hair's-breadth of capsizing and his confidence had been shaken badly.

Jack sagged against the stern as Lily clapped and danced her way back to him.

"We did it!"

"Because of you." He hugged her, closing his eyes to enjoy the feel of her arms about him and her body pressed to his side. Suddenly it wasn't enough.

He drew her before him, staring down, letting her know what he wanted. But this time she didn't run so he pulled her in. Her soft curves molded to his hard planes. She was wet as a seal and cold as the northern river. Her eyelids fluttered closed as she lifted her chin, offering her sweet lips to him again.

His mouth slanted over hers, taking her in a sweeping kiss. His tongue plunged into her mouth, caressing and claiming her.

She clung to his shoulders, her strong fingers digging into his flesh. He wanted to lay her on the deck, strip her bare and make her his.

They thudded into the gunwales. Lily gave a cry of surprise as Jack pressed damp kisses along the cool skin of her neck. Her head fell back and she moaned as he swept her into his arms, his teeth scoring her neck. It was always like this between them, wild and exciting as the rapids.

Some part of Jack's brain registered a scream and shouting. Lily pushed at his shoulders, but it only made him more determined to hold on.

She turned her head, twisting away.

"Jack. Look!"

Chapter Ten

Jack lifted his gaze and followed the direction she indicated. Another boat bobbed out of the canyon. But this one was in more trouble than they had been. The men on board bailed and shrieked. Lily straightened and Jack released her as they both leaned out to watch the unfolding catastrophe.

"They're sinking!"

Jack stared at the half-filled skiff. The men now used their hats to bail, but the vessel continued to dip into the water, sinking by agonizing degrees. Jack took out his oar, making for them against the current in the calm water.

He judged the distance and the speed the skiff sank and knew he would not reach them before they lost the lot.

From behind them came a floating barge, complete

with piles of gear and a fully erected tent. Somehow that craft had shot the rapids unscathed. Jack realized that such a flat conveyance could not take on water or sink. But it could break apart in rough water and it could split into pieces on rocks. The men on the barge steered for the struggling men.

Jack heard a cry and saw the skiff drop below the surface, taken down by a ton of supplies. The men flailed in the icy water as Jack drew beside them. His vessel was stout and he had no fear of them overturning her as they came aboard.

He offered his hand and dragged both passengers in.

One was crying. "Everything. We've lost it all, Cameron."

The other passenger cradled his head in his hands, so at first Jack did not recognize the man who had helped him launch his boat. His heart ached for them as he turned them toward the shore. The two defeated greenhorns would have to hike to the Mounties' outpost at the mouth of the rapids and seek help there, for they had not really lost everything. They still had their lives.

Jack deposited the wet and weeping stampeders on the shore by the portage. Lily and Jack exchanged a look and he knew Lily understood. This could just as easily have been them.

She lingered by the men, patting their shoulders and hovering. Jack noted the Mounties approaching.

"Let's go, Lily."

She glanced up and saw the lawmen and quickly climbed aboard, calling Nala in.

He used the long pole and pushed them back into the gentle current.

They were well in the center before she spoke.

"You built us a strong boat."

"Don't congratulate us just yet. We still have White Horse Rapids."

"Yes, but that's tomorrow's trouble. We are safe and whole today and on our way to Dawson."

Jack rested a hand on the gunwales. "I hope she'll last."

She came to sit beside him at the rudder, nestling close.

"I've watched the building, Jack. Many of those men have no business wielding a hammer much less trying to run rapids. Those two were luckier than most. Because of you, they survived."

"I didn't do anything."

"You turned back."

"Anyone would have."

She sighed and patted his hand as if he were a boy. "No, some would not. It's still a race, Jack. When I imagined this adventure, I recognized the danger, but I never considered seeing so many men fail. It's heartbreaking."

Her teeth chattered and he knew they must get her dry before she got frostbite. He draped the blanket around her and rubbed her shoulders, but she began to shiver, so Jack turned toward shore. He found a nice flat place and was halfway to the landing when he realized the spot was occupied by two men digging.

He and Lily stared as the stampeders heaved a stiff body into a shallow grave. Jack changed the angle of the rudder and with a slow surreal motion, usually reserved for dreams, they drifted by the tableau.

"The river will flood that bank and take them back," said Lily.

Jack made for deeper water, sending them out into the river's gentle flow. How could this be the same river they had battled only minutes ago? He just couldn't get his mind around the change.

"I'll bring us in at the next likely spot and we'll have a fire to warm you up."

"I'll last 'til sunset."

He gave her a hard look and used her words against her.

"And leave a toe or two here? I'll be damned if I'll let your toes turn black, either."

She gave him an approving smile and then disappeared around the front of their gear. Jack thought she meant to spot for hazards, but when several minutes passed, and she didn't appear, he grew worried. He called but received no answer, so he tied the rudder and went forward to check on her.

He rounded the boxes to find her in the bow, her wet clothing stripped off and cast about her. She was naked and crouched, so that he could see her long pale back, narrow waist and lovely pear-shaped bottom. Lily, not yet seeing him, rummaged in her bag, drawing out a white chemise. Jack was so shocked he staggered back against the side with a thud. She turned, giving him a clear view of the full swell of one breast before she clasped the garment to her chest. Her eyes widened and she rose, pressing the chemise tight, but managing only to cover her breasts and sex. She was lovely as a Rubens painting, pink and curvy, with slim arms and tapering legs. Her knees were rosy as her cheeks.

"Who's steering the boat!" she cried.

Jack tried to answer but succeeded only in stammering.

Lily's eyes narrowed and she straightened, looking just as indignant as a woman could. She lifted a slim arm and pointed to the stern. "You get back there."

He retreated, Nala trotting beside him, but the image of Lily, naked, her wet hair curling about her shoulders, stayed fixed in his mind like a beacon. He'd never forget that sight as long as he lived. Her body managed to be earthy and ethereal at the same time as it was sensual and divine. How would he ever look at her again without seeing beneath her clothing?

Jack untied the rudder and kept his eyes on the river while his mind dwelled on her body and all its lush curves and tempting hollows. What lovely contradictions. Slim, yet plump, short yet lithe. The palms of his hands sweated and twitched as he clenched the handle he'd sanded smooth, but not as smooth as her skin.

Lily appeared in his sight shortly thereafter, fully dressed, with a blanket shawl. Her wet clothing was either stowed or hanging aft.

"Don't look at me like that, Jack. I'm not some morsel to be devoured."

He tore his gaze from her, casting it down river and somehow he held it there for several more miles, as Lily hoisted the sails. He did want to devour her—every luscious mouthful.

Jack recognized Squaw Rapids from the white water, but decided that he had better have full light to run them. That would mean they'd take the first tomorrow as a warm-up to the more treacherous White Horse Rapids.

He gazed up at the clear sky, knowing the lack of clouds would bring a cold night. Would she nestle against him again and would he be able to resist her? He knew the temptation would be worse, now that he knew exactly what lay beneath her clothing. He dreaded and anticipated the night in equal measures.

Lily waited until they grounded to slip from the bow and then tied a line about the sturdy trunk of a pine. She secured a second line before joining him. He could tell from the tension in her body that she was struggling as well.

"Are you planning to stare at me all the way to Dawson?" she asked.

He decided to grab the bull by the horns. "Hard not to."

"Well, who asked you to come sneaking around like a peeping Tom?"

"I called. You didn't answer. I was worried."

"A gentleman would have averted his eyes."

"I doubt that."

Lily shoulders sank a little as her pretence of indignation slipped. "You'll not convince me you never saw a woman in the buff before, Jack."

"Never saw one like you, Lil."

She straightened and faced him. Her eyes were wide and glittering. The expression reminded him of grief, but that made no sense. She must still be angry and that was well and good. As long as she was spitting nails, she'd keep her distance and he'd have a fair chance of not following the impulse that was filling his mind even now. But then he recalled their kisses and how she had melted against him. At Lake Bennett she'd asked him not to shame her and he'd tried to do as she asked.

"I've ruined it, haven't I?"

He didn't pretend not to understand her. For it was true. Everything felt different now.

"I can't think of you as just a partner, Lily. Not for a long time now."

"But I'm still your partner."

Jack shook his head. "I want more."

She stared at him with wide troubled eyes.

"You sleep in the boat," he said. "I'll bed down on the bank."

He bailed the boat and then gathered a pile of wood three times what they'd need just to keep away from her as she set out the cooking pan, beans and bacon, just so he could work off some of the steam that now seemed to flow through his veins instead of blood. He was aflame with need and stuck here in the wilderness with a woman who tempted him to distraction, but whom he respected too much to seduce.

He stomped a branch and it splintered, flying in two directions.

He retrieved one and threw it with all his might. It contacted the trunk of a pine and fell to earth, none the worse for his fit of temper. When he finally deemed it safe for him to approach her, he stomped back to camp and dumped the gathered sticks with the rest.

Lily eyed the mountain of fuel and then studied him, but wisely said nothing. Instead, she offered him a full plate of supper. Jack took it and sat apart, staring at the water.

When he finished she took the plate and washed

it with the rest. He watched her arm move in a rhythmic sweep and noted the gentle sway of her hips as she leaned over the water. He gritted his teeth and forced himself to look away as she set everything back to rights. Then she hesitated, standing beside the fire between the boat and where he sat surly as a bear with an infected claw.

"I'm sorry, Jack." Lily didn't move from where she stood, just out of reach, yet near enough that he could smell her fragrant skin. He wanted to roll in that scent until it covered him.

"Go to bed, Lily." *Please go to bed or I'll not be responsible.* He'd never felt the blood-lust so strongly, not even when he was a green lad or when he'd thought himself in love with Nancy. Lily was different, her pull powerful as the moon changing the tides. His instincts told him that bedding her wouldn't solve his dilemma, for he wanted more from her than a tumble. He tried to imagine a life with her—Lily in New York at a dinner party with the Sniders and winced. They wouldn't accept her and he doubted she would accept them.

It wouldn't work, no matter what he wanted. No matter how he pitched it in his mind, he knew that she wouldn't fit in his world, which meant he needed to get her to Dawson and then say goodbye.

Lily stared at him, his arms bunched as he clasped his hands like a man striving to keep from taking what he wanted. The thought of him holding her filled Lily with a simmering desire. She stared at his hands, imagining them cupping her breasts, kneading and stroking. Her body trembled as a sheen of moisture covered her skin. The breeze blew and the temperature dropped with the sun, but she did not feel the cold, for she was warm in the heat of her wanting.

It had been easier back at Lake Bennett, surrounded by thousands of men. The close quarters and complete lack of privacy acted to keep them apart. Jack had his work and she had hers. Now nothing separated them but her certainty that she could have Jack for a day, a week or a season, but never for a lifetime. But she feared that knowing this was not going to stop her from doing something that she would regret. She understood that he would leave her for some fancy white-gloved, New York debutante who had elegant speech and who could run his home in a way that would bring him comfort and pride. Lily's stomach pitched as she imagined the welcome he'd receive if he were foolish enough to bring her home from the Yukon.

It was impossible for her to live a life with no regrets because no matter what she did with Jack, there would be regrets. The only question was which ones? Would she regret loving him and then saying goodbye, or would she regret missing the most memorable adventure of all by turning him away? Despite all her misgivings she wanted him.

A life worth living involved taking chances—did that include risking her heart?

They'd shoot White Horse Rapids tomorrow and there was more than a passing chance they'd drown and be buried in shallow nameless graves with the others. If she knew ahead of time that this would be her last night on earth, what would she do? Her eyes fell on Jack.

She didn't know how it would all end, but she knew she would have him, at least once, for this was an adventure she could not miss, regardless of the danger.

"We've the rapids tomorrow," she said.

He met her steady gaze and nodded, wondering where she was going with this.

"I want to be with you."

"I'll not put you ashore, Lily. You're my partner for good and all."

"That's not what I mean. Tonight, I want to be more than your partner."

He stood in a fluid motion that showed his grace and power. She followed him and met his stern stare with the slightest incline of her head.

He was beside her in an instant and holding her in his arms.

"Are you sure, Lily?"

In answer she lifted her chin and kissed him with

all the passion she had held hostage in her heart. How could she have ever thought that loving this man could shame her? It wouldn't, not ever.

A rain of gentle kisses dropped along her neck, each one sending a shudder through her. His tongue caressed the outer shell of her ear, her knees grew weak and she swayed in his arms. She tilted her head to give him full access to her neck. He traveled its length until he found her willing mouth. Questing lips sought the soft comfort of her own. His mouth slanted across hers, rousing her until her skin burned with inner heat. He held her head, tilting her to accept his kisses as she pressed forward her hips, finding evidence of his need.

His nimble fingers danced over her coat, unfastening her buttons and then his own. He laid the garments on the ground for a bed and then waited for her there. She followed him as she had always followed him, coming to him there upon the wide grassy bank, allowing him to peel away her wrapping until she shivered in her chemise and drawers. His garments followed with none of the slow kisses. She had just a moment to look at him, naked and virile in the fire's glow, his muscles taut, his skin golden and his male member jutting from a nest of dark curls. The sight sent a thrill of excitement through her middle. He retrieved the blanket and lay beside her, bringing the heavy robe up and over them both.

His dark head descended to her bare shoulder,

kissing a trail along the edge of her chemise and releasing the ribbon ties with his teeth. Jack's warm knuckles brushed the swell of her breast and she gasped at the roughness of his skin and the tenderness of his touch.

When his lips touched to one of her nipples, it budded with a pulling tightness that rippled through her middle. His drawing kiss and questing tongue sent pulsating waves rolling to the juncture of her legs. Warmth and wetness spilled from her as she quivered in his caress. The insistent throbbing brought a cry to her lips and she reached instinctively for his hips, splaying her fingers over the taunt muscles of his buttock. His hands left her breasts, stroking her belly with feathery kisses that sent her head spinning. She arched against him, trying to press his big, male body to hers.

She wiggled and strained, wanting him to touch her everywhere at once. His thigh lifted, pinning her legs and then pressing between her thighs. She opened her legs to him, needing him now as much as he needed her. His fingers danced lower, tangling in her tight curls and opening her soft folds.

She tensed at the intimate contact.

"Trust me, Lily. Trust me as you have all this long journey we've taken together."

She closed her eyes and lay back into the warm sheepskin that lined his coat. Jack would take care of her as he always had. His fingers dipped inside her, the slow friction was heaven. On the next stroke, she lifted her hips to meet him.

He kissed her as she rocked gently against his fingers, penetrating her secret places, bringing her a new pleasure. When his thumb began a wonderful circular dance about her swollen flesh, she could not contain the gasps of excitement.

"I can't resist you. You're too sweet."

He shifted, lifting to his forearms as he positioned himself over her. She spread her thighs to make room for him as his hips lowered to meet her own. His fingers withdrew and his male flesh replaced them. He slid into her slowly. Her body was slick, but he was big and the sensation of fullness frightened her. She stopped moving, but he did not, slowly slipping forward, invading her body, taking what she had offered.

As he reached the delicate barrier of her virgin skin her body resisted.

"Lily?" His voice trembled and his body poised, shivering half-sheathed within her. He left the decision to her. Her body pulsed with the need he had roused. She lifted her arms to circle him, clasping his shoulders and sliding the full length of his back, now slick with sweat, until she came to his hips. He held his weight from her, resting on his elbows.

"It will only hurt for a moment."

She nodded and tugged at his hips. He gave a sharp thrust and the fine tissue tore away. His gaze never left hers. Her eyes widened as she felt the barrier release with a tiny tug. An instant later he was fully joined with her.

Was that all—just that little twinge? Lily smiled up at him.

"I'm fine, Jack."

He lowered his head into the hollow of her neck, muffling his words. "Thank God."

Her body needed to move. She rocked tentatively against him. He lifted his head, his expression one she had never seen. He looked wild, excited and possessive all at once. He stared down at her as if she belonged to him.

His hands slipped down and captured her knees, drawing them up until her ankles rested at his shoulders.

"You're mine now."

"Yes," she whispered. "I'm yours."

He clasped her hands, drawing them high above her head. Squeezing her fingers he lifted his hips and then drove forcefully into her body. She locked her ankles about his neck unable to keep herself from lifting to meet the frenzied thrusts that pressed her deep into the folds of his thick coat.

"Wild as the Yukon, just as I imagined," he whispered.

His strokes were velvet, each one building upon the next. Something was happening deep inside her. It started in the place he had first touched her; the pressure of his body in hers and the friction made her ache for more. She threw her head back and spread her thighs wide to bring him deeper as the tension broke, surging through her like white water. She cried out like the wild animal he accused her of being, panting and gasping as her body bubbled with a pleasure that wrung from her a long moan of delight.

"Ah, yes, Lily, that's my girl." He thrust once more and then held them joined together. Deep inside her body, she felt him move, though his body was still and then came a rush of liquid from his body to hers. He groaned and fell upon her, collapsing with a completeness that would have frightened her had she not felt the same lethargy. They had energy only to lie together, slick with sweat and panting from their exertions.

He enfolded her in his arms, carrying her with him as he rolled from her and onto his side with his face pressed tightly in the lea of her neck.

Within her body she felt his flesh slipping from hers and sighed with frustration at losing the connection between them. She stroked his head, listening to his soft breathing as he fell asleep in her arms. Sometime in the night, he roused to place more wood on the fire, slipping into his clothing. The night was cold, so she did the same, lacing her chemise and drawing on her bloomers, finding a tightness in her legs. She gave a little groan.

"Did I hurt you?" he asked.

"No. My muscles are sore, is all."

He stroked his big hand over her hair and smiled down at her. "Only natural."

Lily returned his smile as he gathered her up in his arms, warming her again. She stared up at the sky, but the gray clouds kept her from seeing the stars. She felt herself falling asleep, wishing she could sleep beside Jack every day for the rest of her life. She didn't regret what they had done. It was beautiful and right.

Chapter Eleven

The whine of mosquitoes woke Lily. She opened her eyes to find Jack standing far down the bank at the water's edge with Nala who was fetching a stick he threw out into the river.

She smiled at the picture they made, as if he were a boy with his dog instead of a man about to fight the river once more. She stretched and felt a twinge of sore muscles at her thighs. A glance showed a small smear of dried blood there. It was not time for her monthly courses, so she wrinkled her brow a moment as she stared. Had he torn something inside her?

The blood had ceased so whatever it was had passed. Lily washed herself with a wet rag and icy river water and then dressed.

As she slipped into her woolen stockings, and added layer upon layer to her outer garments, she remembered the sweetness of their joining and the words he'd whispered. *You're mine now, Lily.* But what did that mean?

She wasn't. Couldn't be if he was to have his dream. And he wasn't fool enough to bring home a poor Irish wife. Choosing her would make him an outcast, hold him back in his aim to return triumphant to New York. And even if he did ask her to come with him, her dreams of adventure did not include living in a city known for its hatred of the Irish or being snubbed by all Jack's high-class friends.

There was the rub. If she let him go, he could live his dream and she could live hers. But if they stayed together, they'd face a mean choice; to have each other, they'd have to forego all they had fought and struggled for. They would have to give up their dreams.

Lily thought of her mother, as she buttoned her coat. "I understand now, Ma, why you took those men to your bed. But you made me promise the impossible. You can't live a life without regrets, though sometimes you get to choose which ones to live with."

This morning she was brimming with remorse, because she'd tasted what it could be like between them and now she must let him go. Once was a risk. More than that was foolishness. She'd wind up like her mother, pregnant and alone. She doubted the saloons in Dawson would hire her then. Her entire grim future stretched out before her. Repeating her mother's mistakes, walking the same tired treadmill.

No. It had to stop. He was a man, so he'd want more of her. That meant she needed to remind Jack of his dreams and responsibilities. He had obligations to his family and they came before her.

She couldn't cost him everything that he'd fought and struggled for. Lily closed her eyes against the pain of what she must do.

A life worth living, her mother had said. A life without regret. Lily hung her head and wept.

Jack walked back along the shore toward the curling fire of their camp. Lily was up. He smiled as memories of last night mingled with anticipation of seeing her again.

"Find Lily," he said to her hound and pointed.

Nala trotted off, head high, stick clamped in her mouth. Jack watched Nala drop the stick upon the ground beside her mistress. Jack wished he had something to give Lily, as well.

Lily grabbed Nala around the neck and hugged her tight, burying her face in the big dog's neck.

Jack slowed. Something was wrong. He set off again now with greater speed. When he reached her, she did not look up, keeping her eyes fixed on the frying bacon, worrying the thick strips unnecessarily with a fork.

"Lily?"

She waved at the mosquitoes but did not look at him. He dropped to his knees beside her and waited, hands pressed to his thighs. He had a sick feeling in his stomach. Had he hurt her?

"What's wrong?"

She lifted her free hand and pressed it to her mouth as if to keep from crying. Blue eyes shone from within red-rimmed lids. A knife blade of anxiety sliced across his middle. Why wouldn't she speak to him?

"It was a mistake, Jack."

"No. It wasn't. We're perfect together."

She shook her head, covering her eyes with the palms of both hands. "We have to stop. It's not right, what we're doing."

Was this about sin, then? She was Catholic and such things prayed heavy on the spirit. After all they weren't married.

He opened his mouth to reassure her and then stopped. He wanted Lily, more than he'd ever wanted a woman. But how could he have her? How could he bring her back to New York and make her a laughingstock?

She met his gaze now, her expression hard and her eyes wise. She waited and then he recognized that she understood all this already, had worked it all out, while it was only just hitting him. He couldn't marry her, not if he was to return to the life he left. Not if he was going to do as he promised and return his mother to society and see his sister educated and well wed, to give them back the life they had lost. Was he a cad to still want those things?

And what about Lily? What did she want?

He'd taken a virgin. He had a duty to her now as well.

"I'll marry you," he said, his voice no more than a whisper as if that was all the breath he could muster.

Her eyes widened, but the lines about her mouth remained hard.

"What about your sister and your ma?"

"I'll send them what money I can."

"No, Jack. It's a generous offer. But I'll not cost you everything."

He couldn't meet her eyes.

"They'll never accept me."

"I know that."

"It won't work. We're too different you and I. And we want different things."

He swallowed the lump that seemed to be rising like bread dough in his throat. His eyes began to sting.

"You're smart, Jack. I don't have to explain how the world works to you. Right now it's only about you and me. If we go on, there'll be a baby to reckon with."

He nodded his understanding, taking a moment before he spoke. "I'm sorry Lily. I never meant to hurt you."

"I know that." She turned back to the fire, serving out his breakfast and handing it to him. He accepted the plate certain that he would not be able to swallow.

His heart ached with the grief over what he had done. Until Lily, he'd never had a female friend, one he could confide in. And now he had destroyed the trust and very likely their friendship. Lily should have been wedded and bedded by a husband who loved her, instead of being taken on a wild river by a man half crazed by lust.

If he had known it was her first time he never would have… It was a lie.

Jack felt his heart bleed with guilt and shame. He was a fool.

Lily packed up the camp while Jack set the sail. When she finally climbed aboard with Nala, she moved to the bow without looking at him.

He was about to push off, but instead he stood on the muddy beach, eyes on Lily, where she stood gazing out like the figurehead of a ship.

"Will we still be friends?" he asked.

Lily filled with a deep, welling sadness as she looked at him. Regret, she realized, for what she still wanted and could not have. "We're partners until Dawson, Jack. Just as we promised. Now cast us off."

He did, releasing the lines and pushing the boat off the bank, then climbing aboard.

If she had known that her choice to lay with Jack would include this hollow, dry ache, would she still have done it? Lily stared out at the river scanning for obstacles. Here it was all so plain. She could see the dangers and move to avoid them. But with Jack, it was different.

It was not until they were sucked into Squaw Rapids, that Lily came from her musings. The surging white water forced her to focus on what was before her. Perhaps if she could just keep looking ahead, just as far as she could see, she could get through this.

She found the speed more exhilarating than terrifying. But the rush of water and blur of the shore did not make her forget Jack's words. *You're mine, now.* And afterward, *I'm sorry, Lily.* They played over and over in her mind. She had other regrets as well, among them she regretted her own stupidity at bringing such a wedge between them now when they needed to pull together more than ever.

Lily stared at the cliffs rising up from the rocky bank, her stomach churning like the water at its base. This was the passage that everyone feared and word was that there were many new graves on the banks beyond the canyon.

She looked back to see Jack turn the rudder, making for the bank. He'd said he would study the water from the cliffs and watch some others try to shoot the rapids before they took their turn.

It showed wisdom. Jack was a cautious man, usually, but not where she was concerned. Had she made a mistake loving him? Her head said yes, but her heart longed to hold him again. If they didn't reach Dawson soon she might fall back into the same trap.

They scraped the rocky bank. Jack left her to watch their belongings so he could hike to the portage on his scouting mission. While he was gone a smooth-cheeked Mountie came poking about.

He copied down the number they'd painted on the bow.

"You two planning to portage, ma'am?"

"No, we'll run them."

"No, ma'am. You'll walk around. The boat can go through with the others."

She'd said they had four men aboard, including her husband.

"But you're required by law to portage."

"Oh, well then, that's what I'll be doing, of course. I'd not want to break the law."

"They can hire a pilot. We've a list of qualified men."

"Hire? Oh, I'll ask them to do so. Worth the money, I'm sure."

"Better safe than sorry." He tipped his wide-brimmed hat and marched off like a police officer. Most of her encounters with such men involved being told she couldn't sleep here or rest there or dawdle on this corner—and here they were, still ordering her about. *Move along, move along.*

Lily settled down to watch the river knowing she'd

do as she liked and no man, uniformed or otherwise, would tell her different, for this was her adventure for good or bad.

She understood the risks, but she'd not leave Jack blind on the most dangerous stretch of water from here to Dawson.

Lily turned her gaze to the river. All the men that passed looked exactly the same, grim and wide-eyed. She noticed one man, small, with a dark hat and full beard. Her Brooklyn tailor.

"Mr. Luritz!" She waved frantically and called again.

He turned and spotted her.

"Miss Shanahan!" He waved back. "I haven't forgotten your dresses!"

She cupped her hands over her mouth. "Good luck!"

He waved again and then held on to his hat as the boat picked up speed. Lily whispered a prayer for him.

She watched until his flat barge disappeared, dropping from sight as if it had fallen off the edge of the earth. Lily wondered at the drop, for he had vanished, mast and all. The parade of crafts continued through the afternoon. Jack came back before dark. He was uncharacteristically quiet.

"It's that bad?" she asked.

He nodded his head.

"Jack, I don't like secrets so you'd best tell me."

"I saw three boats go down."

"A flat barge?"

Jack wrinkled his brow. "Yes. One like that hit the rocks and broke apart. But Lil, I saw two other barges make it through."

Had Luritz crossed safely?

"Another craft capsized. They were all drowned. Seven men." He shook his head. "Another took on too much water and sank. I hope we're not overloaded. I've calculated the height of the sides, but I never saw water boil like that."

"Mounties came by and took our number."

Jack looked somber. "They told you that you needed to walk."

She nodded.

"They're checking all passengers, Lily, and they're checking the boats."

"Then I'll need a pair of pants and a good hat."

Jack stared a moment and then spoke in a low, scratchy voice. "If anything should happen to you, I'll never forgive myself."

"Jack, you need me. I'm your eyes."

"I don't want you aboard."

She glared. "I'm your partner to Dawson. You agreed."

He tried unsuccessfully to stare her down and then nodded once. "All right. But if they stop you, you'll walk."

Lily had a horrible image of watching from above

as Jack struck a rock he did not see. But she accepted his hand and shook.

"Deal."

He didn't let her go. She didn't pull away. The heat between them blazed anew.

"Jack?"

"It's bad water, Lily. Real bad."

She nodded and squeezed tight to his hand. "We'll make it through. You've built the best boat on the river."

His grin was lopsided, but his eyes remained troubled. She released his hand and hugged him. His arms came about her hard and fast, clasping her tight. She felt the tension in him and the strength. What would she give to be a New York debutante?

"We'll make it, Jack. I just know it."

She thought she felt him kiss the top of her head before he set her aside.

"'Course we will." His eyes glittered.

Lily wondered at the horrors he'd seen this day and was glad she did not have those pictures bobbing about in her mind.

Lily washed and packed her gear as Jack scattered the coals on the rocks. Then he waited on the bank as she changed into a pair of dungarees that fitted her round bottom a little too snugly. The old work shirt was torn at the hem, but covered her curves. She tugged on a battered old hat and regarded him from beneath the brim.

"Well?"

Her skin was too fair and flawless to fool anyone at close quarters. But from a distance she might pass for a boy.

"Where did you get those?" he asked.

"Traded for them."

He cast a disparaging look at her attire. "I think you were robbed."

She stared up at him. "Ready?"

The Mounties checked them in a little farther down river. Lily stayed with the boat and kept her head down. Afterward they waited on the bank for their turn behind two canoes, an overloaded skiff and a barge complete with tent and stove.

"My, they'd never have to go ashore," said Lily admiring the practicality of the craft.

"Unless the lashing fails and they break apart."

They proved prophetic words, for the barge operator was clumsy and as Lily and Jack watched them from the bank they failed to make the turn after the landings, crashing immediately into the boulders before the 300-foot bluff of black basalt now directly before them. Lily gasped as the barge lifted, spilling the men into the water, their tent crumpling as the stove dragged it into the river. She could not hear the logs break, but she could see them separating like the stays of a fan as the goods fell through the cracks.

Two men scrambled to the shore, but the others were swept along.

Lily turned her worried eyes on Jack.

"Improper rudder," he said.

The skiff went next, turning neatly round the bend to the left and out of sight. The canoes went together and then it was their turn.

Chapter Twelve

A whistle brought Nala into the boat and a few moments later they joined the other vessels pulled downriver by an ever-increasing current.

The river began gently enough. Jack spotted the red flag on the pole and the sign announcing they were in the canyon. He knew before he reached the looming cliffs that the river would be forced to a hard left. Jack also knew from his scouting that there was a reef on the left bank, a mad tangle of logs and rocks, but the cliffs lay to the right with the faster water. Where he placed them was all. He had decided to hug close to the reef to put them in a better central position as they took the next right angle through the canyon. Lily had worked out sign language that mainly involved her pointing to hazards and then waving to clear water. She spied the reef, as sure as any springer spaniel spotting game, and waved him right, but he took them close then turned the rudder with all he had. The water roared like a maelstrom and pulsed like the heart of a great serpent. He hugged the horse's mane of white water, shooting out into the canyon. Lily noticed the reef a quarter mile downriver and pointed. The most dangerous part of their journey rushed at him with inhuman speed. The reef further pinched the churning water into five-foot waves.

She motioned to the right and he leaned, fighting the rush of water that tried to snatch the rudder away. The waves beat against the sides and splashed over the deck, knocking Lily down. She righted herself as he held them in position. Just then the boat pitched as if some sea monster had hit them from below. Not a rock, he knew, but the waves, tossing them up and then leaving them airborne an instant before they crashed back to the river.

Lily's feet left the deck. Jack stared in horror as she seemed to move in slow motion, flying up into the air as if catapulted. She sailed over the side and into the white water.

"Lily," he howled, but the roar ate his words. He searched the water, but saw nothing.

Nala leapt over the side, disappearing after her mistress.

Jack shot past the reef, hitting the widening river and the slowing water. He leaned over the gunwale, looking for Lily. Her hat bobbed along, but he could not see her.

"Lily!" He could hear his voice now and the splashing.

He ran to the bow. There they were.

Nala swam nose in the air, thrashing her forelegs at the water. Lily clutched her dog round her thick neck and Jack found he could breathe again.

"I got you."

Nala changed direction, making for the boat instead of the shore. He reached for an oar and extended it to Lily. She clasped hold of the pole and he dragged her to the side. Jack hauled Lily up first and then the two of them tugged her dog out of the water.

With his girls safe, Jack staggered back. Lily sank down beside him and Jack grasped her, dragging her into his arms.

"I nearly lost you," he whispered, pressing his cheek to the top of her wet head.

"No, I'm here."

He closed his eyes at the joy of it. The shock of her fall brought home just how much he needed Lily. She was more than his partner. More than the object of his desire.

"Thank God."

"And thank my hound." Lily patted Nala who had already shaken off and lay at her mistress's feet.

Jack squeezed her tight and kissed her wet, cold

lips, warming them with his own. There was a whooping cry from close beside them.

She drew back and stroked his cheek, pride beaming from her over what they had accomplished together.

Jack pushed his hat back on his head.

"We did it," he said, grinning at her.

"We sure did." She held her smile until it became brittle.

He stood and offered his hand, she let him pull her to her feet, then she stepped away. The moment was gone and he'd lost her again.

"Damn, boys, we've shot them rapids!"

Lily popped her head over the edge of the hull. He followed her example to see a skiff with two men, one at each oar, drift past them toward the many sandbars to the left of the widening river.

"We made it, Jack. Dawson's only a hop and skip from here."

Actually they were yet to reach the halfway mark. But they would be on the river for all of it and the Chilkoot Pass, their first winter and now the White Horse Rapids all lay behind them.

"Damned if we didn't," he said.

"I've got to change. Go to the back again and don't come forward unless I call for you."

He nodded and did as she bid him, knowing what would happen if he didn't. Since their night together, he had kept his hands off her, but not his mind. He watched her at the bow, taking in every nuance and each gesture. He watched her by the firelight when she slept. And now, as he knew she was changing, he remembered that day he had seen her there, savoring the memories as a starving man recalls a feast. He had not stopped wanting Lily, had accepted long ago and many miles back that he'd never stop.

Lily did not forget the sight of the fresh graves beyond the White Horse Canyon or the icy bite of the river after she had been pitched in. So she stayed well back as they took Five Fingers Rapids, named for the fingerlike rocks that jutted up from the river. Lily thought the black humps of rock looked like the body of the whale that ate Jonah.

They made it past Big Salmon and Little Salmon, through the community of Sixty Mile, so named for its distance from Fort Yukon. They camped on the river when possible to discourage the mosquitoes that now flew in black clouds on the shore. Jack had rigged a metal-and-brick floor in the boat as a platform for cooking. She set their fires in a metal basin that Jack would use for a wheelbarrow once in Dawson. As daylight stretched to eighteen hours a day and the river grew calm, she suggested they work in shifts, each sailing the boat for six hours and then resting. This brought them to Dawson City on July 4, 1898.

Lily stood beside Jack at the stern as they sailed

the last two miles along the wide river, flanked by green pine on one side and the white-capped mountains of The Dome on the other.

"It's a fine way to celebrate Independence Day," said Lily.

"But we're in Canadian territory," Jack reminded her.

Lily waved off his observation as she studied the shore. There were many cabins, each with nice piles of dirt just waiting to be sorted.

"What are those? They look like wooden gutters in the stream." She asked pointing at a series of wooden troughs set beside the tributaries leading out to the river.

"That's a Long Tom. It's kind of an extended rocker box. You feed the dirt into the top and then rock it like a cradle. The stream water running through and the rocking washes away the dirt and gravel leaving the heavier material, including the gold, to be trapped in the riffles."

She stared in wonder at the filthy man who threw shovelful after shovelful into the top of the contraption.

Jack pointed. "At the bottom are small slats of wood that trap the heaviest material and gold is heavier than any other thing out here."

Lily craned her neck as they sailed on, wishing she could see to the bottom of that trough. Next came a little inlet which held hundreds of logs, just waiting for the sawmill. Two horses ate hay from a trough made from a canoe and everywhere freshly sawn planks covered half-constructed buildings.

"That's it. Dawson City," said Jack as he turned the rudder.

Lily studied the rough collection of structures, looking for the biggest and grandest of them all, for that was where she planned to work.

"We should stay on the boat a few nights," said Jack, who had become more and more sullen as they neared their destination.

"We'll see," she said, not wanting to be alone in the boat with him, knowing they would separate afterward, knowing their parting would make her more apt to forget all the reasons that sleeping with him was such a bad idea.

As it happened, Lily was offered a job the day she set foot in Dawson, singing at the Pavilion, an arrangement that included a shared room at a boarding house and board at one of the hotels. She also rented a five-by-five piece of warehouse space, so Jack could search for a claim on which to try his invention without worrying about his supplies.

She came to the boat when the last of his gear was stowed in the guarded warehouse and handed him a billfold.

"What's this?" he asked.

"It's $428.00, your half of what we earned since we partnered up." She extended the money, waiting.

"Thank you, partner."

She held on to the wallet a moment too long. "You won't go spending it in the gambling halls, will you?"

"I'm a Baptist, Lily."

"What has that to do with squandering money?"

"We don't drink and we don't gamble."

"Are you funning me?"

He shook his head. "No, ma'am."

"I never heard of a man not drinking or gambling." She glanced about. "I hope there aren't too many other Baptists around here."

"I wouldn't worry."

She returned her attention to him. "Will you come see my first show? Just for luck?"

Jack shook his head, feeling the ache already gripping his heart. Their parting had come.

"I'm heading up Bonanza Creek. I hear there is a claim or two for sale there that's played out. Might be able to buy it now." He held up the wallet.

Lily toyed with the lace collar of her best blouse. "The owner of the Pavilion says all the good claims were gone before the fall and all that's left is grubstakes, working for those that own the claims."

He patted her cheek. "Don't worry, Lily. I'll not starve."

She clasped his hand and held it to her cheek, closing her eyes for a moment. When she opened them, they glistened. At first he thought it was her frequent temper, but then he realized it was tears. Lily was close to crying.

Her voice broke and she tried a second time to speak. “Well, if you do come back, come to the Pavilion. I haven’t forgotten my promise to look out for you all I can.”

She released his hand and they stood suddenly awkward in the street. They had been through so much and he had grown to care for her.

“A hauler offered me five hundred dollars for Nala. I turned him down.” She looked worried. “I’ve a favor to ask, Jack. I don’t want her stolen while I’m working. Will you take her for a while? They won’t let me keep her at the boarding house and she likes you.”

“I’d be glad to have her.”

“Don’t sell her.”

“Never. And I’ll bring her to see you when I’m in town for supplies.”

He felt the time between them slipping away.

Had she given him Nala to protect her dog or to insure she would see him again? He stared at her lovely face and wondered why he could not think of anything important to say.

“You were a good partner, Lily.”

She smiled, but then her chin trembled and he thought he’d said the wrong thing again.

“I never had much luck with men, Jack. Hard to trust them, you know. But you kept your word. And

I thank you. And I'll not say goodbye, for you're coming to see me with Nala. Promise."

He nodded, finding a lump in his throat prevented him speaking. Once he had wanted to be rid of her and now that he was, he found he was not ready to let her go. He hoped she'd kiss him, but she didn't.

Lily hugged him, pressing her lovely face into his dirty coat. He stroked her hair and lowered his chin to breathe in her fragrance once more. Then she pulled back and called Nala. The hound came, but her tail was down and she looked to her mistress.

"Go on, Nala." Lily motioned her away.

Jack turned and headed for the river. He couldn't look back, because if he did he'd do something foolish. Nala somehow sensed that Lily would not be coming with them and she whined anxiously.

Jack felt his shoulders sag. The weight of the journey, the sorrow of their parting and the uncertainty of his future all preyed upon him.

Would his invention even work?

Chapter Thirteen

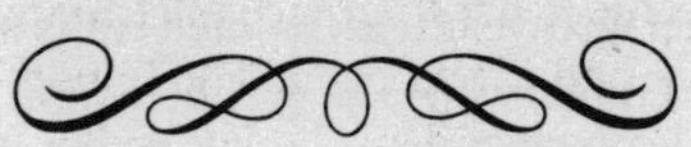

Lily could not have asked for a better start. Before the week was up she was the object of a war between the Pavilion and the Forks. The Forks had a piano, but the Pavilion offered her a better wage. After hearing her sing, the owner of the Pavilion, Donald Trost, was determined not to lose her. He was stocky, with a ruddy complexion and a nose for business. They were much alike in that and she enjoyed negotiating with a man who knew how it was done. He managed to get her exclusively and for six nights a week, with a second show on Saturday nights. In return she arranged to receive a small percentage of the house, plus she did not have to drink with the customers or dance with them. The large hall had a stage where she performed nightly, with the exception of Sundays, when the Mounties shut down all such establishments. They also forbade the carrying of firearms and kept the stampeders in tight check. Because of them, Dawson City was far safer and more orderly than San Francisco had been.

The Pavilion was just a sawboard hall, rough-hewn and still smelling of sawdust, but the stage was wide with kerosene lamps all along the edge and a real curtain. She had high hopes that there would be a grand hotel next year with painted walls and a fine chandelier. Goods would be arriving soon by ferry.

Lily planned to stay as long as the gold, longer perhaps, for she loved it here. The men and women she met all shared her thirst for adventure and impressed her daily with their toughness. And if that were not enough to recommend this territory, the scenery was like none she'd ever imagined, and it was populated by such wondrous creatures. She'd seen a moose with two calves on the bank at Forty Mile.

Wouldn't it be wonderful to make a life in the north and grow with the territory? There was hope here and people willing to work hard to succeed—all kinds of people from all over the country and the world. It baffled and thrilled her.

Her first Saturday night was standing-room only. When the Mounties threatened to shut them down, Trost limited the number of entrants, which allowed the barmaids to get through the mob to bring them beer.

It was on the second Saturday that the first greenhorn threw a small sack of gold dust at her feet. For that she blew him a kiss. It was not the first bag or the first kiss.

Her only regret was that Jack did not come. Three weeks already and she had not seen him or her dog. She wanted him to hear her sing and see how the men cheered and stomped their feet. Somehow it mattered to her that he witnessed her success.

Lily had to admit that she had entertained worries that Jack would become like the men her mother had brought home as soon as they reached Dawson, using her for the warm bed, free food and pocket money she could provide. But it seemed the opposite was true. He didn't need her for anything and that troubled her more than she had thought possible, for she still needed him.

The little tailor had arrived, hat in hand, but he reported having had to hock his scissors in order to eat. Lily went with him to retrieve them and then buy fabric. She allowed him to use her room when she was on the stage. Within the week, Luritz had made her two new dresses. One was pale pink with a tight bodice of satin and a frothy full skirt. The color complemented her pale skin and made her cheeks look rosy. The second was a heavy black velvet gown that matched her hair. During the final fitting, her tailor's stomach gave a loud growl.

She eyed him suspiciously. "When did you last eat, Mr. Luritz?"

He hung his head. "I can't find a mine owner to take me. Too little and too old, they say. But I wasn't too little to climb those mountains."

Jack had been right—all profitable claims were staked, leaving the newcomers without hope of mining their own land. Mine owners had their pick of the thousands that poured in from the lakes. Here, as back there, men had no work.

She'd never been in a situation where she had plenty while others went without, and she found she didn't like it. She might not be able to feed them all, but she could feed this man. Lily went to her dresser, brought back the remains of her unfinished breakfast that held thinly sliced toast and strawberry jam and offered it to her tailor.

"Here, Mr. Luritz."

His face colored, but he took it and ate it with a frightening speed. She remembered what it was to be that hungry. It devoured a person's pride.

"Mr. Luritz, I have need of another outfit." Two was actually more than she'd ever had or needed, but she had the gold and he needed it. "Not for the stage. A skirt with matching jacket. Are you up to the task?"

"Yes, yes."

"You're hired. Come back tomorrow morning at

nine. We'll have breakfast together and then go get the fabric."

He tipped his hat, showing the second strange circular hat beneath. "You're a good lady, Miss Lily."

Then he left her. She watched him out the window as he crossed the street, wearing no gloves. Had he lost them on the journey or sold them?

That afternoon she went to buy men's gloves. While she was out she spoke to every woman she could find about what a job Luritz had done on her gowns. Dolly Isles and Felicity Volmer, who both boarded at the same hotel, asked her to have him come round to see them, for the women in Dawson found no shortage of opportunities to earn a living.

Just before showtime, she tracked down Donald Trost, finding him in his office and asked him for the use of the smaller storeroom behind the stage.

He didn't even glance up from his ledger. "For what?"

"A tailor shop."

"I'm using it."

"The tailor will pay you eight percent of his profits for rent. You'll make money, Donny."

"I like when you call me Donny." He was on his feet now, smiling at her. It seemed an expression he had not much experience with. "All right, then."

Lately she'd found him staring at her more and more, and not in the way a man looks at his cash cow. It made her wary.

He dropped the pencil and slapped the account book closed, then stood and tugged on his vest. He stepped out from around his desk, leaning back against the edge and held out a hand. She didn't want to take it. He was too damned big and experience had told her to stay clear of a man's reach. But he'd never threatened her, so she pushed back her uncertainty and accepted his hand.

"You know I'm fond of you, Lily. Very fond." He lifted her hand to his lips. His mouth was dry and his cheek as coarse as sandpaper.

She resisted the urge to tug free. Out in the hall, the fiddler began tuning with a familiar plucking. Trost couldn't keep her long. It would be bad for business.

"I've been thinking about you. We'd make a good team, you and I. I'd like to start seeing you, Lily. What say you to that?"

She knew this game. You didn't need to pay a wife a salary, for she had to work for free and she could not quit. Lily was certain Trost would like that situation, while she would not. Now, how to stall him indefinitely and still keep her job?

She retrieved her hand. "I think that if I'm not on that stage for the opening number my boss will fire me."

He laughed at that and she made it to the door.

"Running won't help, Lily. I'm a determined man."

That last comment sounded more threat than promise.

The fiddler began and she stepped to the center stage, waiting for the workmen to draw back the curtain. Her performance went on without a hitch. The curtain was drawn and she stooped to collect the two small bags of gold dust thrown by admirers, tucking them in her bodice.

A frantic barking caused her to turn toward the stairs. Her dog pushed through the curtain, nose down as she followed Lily's scent.

"Nala!"

Her dog lifted her head and spotted Lily, then began a wild yipping and twisting.

Lily stooped to rub the dog's belly and stroke her head. Nala righted herself and rested her head on Lily's shoulder.

"Oh, Nala, I've missed you," she whispered as she hugged her dog.

"Still feed her once a day, all she can eat."

She glanced up at the familiar voice to see Jack, now clean-shaven and looking tall and handsome with a new confidence that seemed to surround him like a halo. Her heart rate surged and before she knew it she was lunging toward him. He scooped her up in his arms and turned her in a wide, sweeping circle.

"Oh, Jack, you terrible man. Where have you been?"

He laughed and set her down.

"Working—though I'll say you seem to be better at extracting gold than I am." He laughed and the sound warmed her inside and out.

"Did you hear me sing?" She could not keep the excitement from her voice.

"You're like an angel. They're all in love with you."

All but him, she thought, and was unsettled at the pang of regret.

She took a good long look at him, filling herself with the pleasure of being beside him again, then taking in the changes. He looked thin and tired.

"Have you eaten?"

"You going to make me some of your biscuits and bacon?"

"I can do better than that." She drew out one of the bags of dust and dangled it before him like a watch on a chain. "I'll buy us both a steak."

He grinned. "Sharing supper, just like old times."

"It was less than a month ago, Jack."

He nodded. "Seems longer."

She felt a tugging at her heart. It was that way for her, too. Had he missed her? She prayed so, for it would be such agony to be alone in her torment.

She linked arms with him and led him out, stopping for the wolf skin cloak she'd purchased. At the restaurant she paid for three dinners, so Nala could have salmon and rice. Nala finished first, of course.

Over dinner Lily learned Jack had a claim that had panned out for the last miner, but that he was digging in, following what he thought was a promising old stream bed. The deal included a rough cabin, but he'd had little time to make improvements.

"My machine's up and running and it works, Lily. I only need to engage investors and then I can produce and sell the machines to the mine owners."

"It works?"

"Better than I had hoped. I'd love to show it to you, Lily. I want you to see what I've done."

The excitement in his voice warmed her heart nearly as much as the knowledge that her opinion still mattered to him.

She reached across the table to lay her hand upon his. "I'm so proud of you."

A moment later he had hers captured between both of his hands. "You haven't even seen it yet."

"I know you, Jack. If anyone can build a gold-digging machine, it's you."

His thumb stroked over the skin on the back of her hand. Her reaction to the tiny caress struck her with a force that caused her to inhale sharply. She felt her stomach tighten and her skin flush. Lily drew her hand away before she did something or said something that would embarrass them both. His absence had been hard on her, so hard that she'd nearly forgotten his plans to make his fortune and leave her behind.

"I have a canoe," he said. "We can make it in less than an hour."

Say no, Lily. Tell him you have plans. Tell him that you've moved on. But what she heard herself say was, "I'm off tomorrow."

He grinned. "I'll pick you up for breakfast. Dress in your old clothes."

"I still have them."

He walked her to her door and waited. She wondered what he'd do if she kissed him goodbye? The possibility started her heart on a mad thumping that made her positively dizzy. Try as she might, she could not keep from casting glances at his mouth as she recalled their night together.

There were men everywhere here and yet she could think of only one, one that didn't want her. And *that* made her a damn fool.

He paused before a door that led up the back stairs to her room.

"I can't wait for you to see my system. I don't think I'll sleep tonight. Of all the stampeders in Dawson, you're the one whose opinion I value. If you think I've got something, I know I do."

Was her opinion all he wanted from her? She had so much more she could give him. But no matter what she did or how successful she was here, she couldn't turn herself into the kind of woman he sought.

"I swear if you'd been at my father's side you'd never have let him invest in those railroad stocks."

She wanted to be by Jack's side. She lowered her head, plucking aimlessly at the rabbit fur of her muff.

He clasped her chin between his thumb and index finger, lifting her gaze to meet his. "Thank you for the meal."

She held her breath, hoping he would kiss her again. She knew she was a fool, but she didn't care. She wanted to feel his lips again, inhale the fragrance of wood shavings and smoke and tangle her fingers in his thick hair.

She leaned in, kissing his cheek as he did the same. She closed her eyes against the bitter disappointment. Didn't he want to kiss her?

"Lily?" The voice came from behind her.

She broke away from Jack and turned to see Don Trost scowling at the two of them.

Her boss stood in the evening sunshine, his posture erect, his fists clenched. Jack, by contrast, leaned casually against the door frame, scratching Nala behind the ears.

"Jack Snow, this is Don Trost, owner of the Pavilion."

Jack wisely decided to nod rather than shake. Don continued to scowl. Lily's caution turned to annoyance.

"Was there something you wanted?" she asked Don.

"I couldn't find you after the show. Alexander said you stepped out with a greenhorn."

Lily tapped her foot. "And?"

Don glared at Jack then turned his attention back to Lily. "You never accept invitations from the men. I was worried."

Some of her ire melted, until she began to question his motives.

"Jack's my old partner. We were just…catching up."

Don had seen them kiss, but he had no claim on her. She hadn't even agreed to see him. Still he had a murderous glint in his eye. Lily had witnessed enough street fights to recognize when one was brewing.

She waited for him to decide if he would fight Jack. The two were evenly matched in size, and she knew that despite the ban on firearms, Don carried a small pistol in his pocket. She'd seen him in action and knew he didn't fight fair. Jack likely would follow some Princeton code of sportsmanship and get himself shot.

"Well if you're done reminiscing, I'll take you in."

Ah, now that was a problem. If she accepted, Don would think he had some claim on her and if she didn't she'd leave them to themselves, which was a bad idea. Two tomcats should never be left alone in an alley.

Jack conceded his claim with an ease that nearly broke her heart. "See you tomorrow, Lily."

Didn't he care what she did or who she did it with? That realization struck her like a punch to her middle. She watched him go with a mixture of despair and longing.

Jack held a pleasant smile and replaced his hat before calling to Nala, who left her side to trot off with Jack. That second betrayal brought enough water to her eyes to blur her vision.

Don did not wait for Jack to disappear before confronting her. "Just what kind of a partnership was this exactly?"

"What's that supposed to mean?"

"Lily, I'm not blind. I saw the way you looked at him."

Had Jack seen?

Don clasped Lily's upper arm and tugged her forward, causing her to stumble against him.

Lily saw Jack retrace his steps toward her. His smile was gone and his gaze was fixed on the place where Don clenched her forearm.

Nala was quicker. The dog shot forward, teeth bared, and leapt on Don, taking him to the ground.

Lily swiftly grabbed her dog's collar and pulled her off. Don aimed his pistol at Nala. She stepped between them and glared.

"You'd best go, Don."

Trost stood, mud now clinging to his back and

fine trousers. His face was pink as the inside of a prize-winning watermelon and his expression had turned murderous. He kept his eyes on Jack as he lowered the pistol.

Lily placed a hand on his wrist. "Take yourself off or tomorrow you will find yourself a new singer."

That seemed to break his concentration.

His eyes flicked to her for an instant and then back to Jack.

She squeezed his wrist. "I mean it."

He shook her off and her hand came away muddy. "We've a contract."

"That says I leave when I want."

He spun and stormed down the boardwalk, his heels pounding an angry rhythm on the planking.

Lily's shoulders sagged and she turned back to Jack to find him glaring at her.

"Does he have some claim on you?"

"No."

Jack nodded, but his expression stormed like a rain cloud.

"If he bothers you, you let me know."

Lily smiled. He cared enough to defend her and that counted for something.

Lily smiled. "He's just protecting his investment."

"And what is he to you?"

"My boss, of course."

"Is that all?"

"For now." Oh, he didn't like that answer, not

judging from the lowering of his brows and the thinning of his lips. Lily felt happier than she had in days. "I'll see you at breakfast, Jack."

Chapter Fourteen

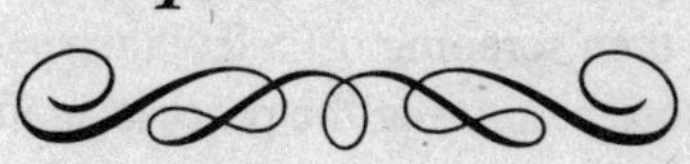

Lily met Luritz in the parlor of the boardinghouse to deliver instructions to eat at the hotel without her, then buy the yardage for her garments and meet her tomorrow morning at the Pavilion. She was excited to show him the little storeroom in which he could set up shop and knew there was much potential business here repairing clothing and producing new garments. With luck, he'd be headed home to his beautiful daughters before the snow began to fly.

Jack arrived shortly thereafter and they set out, reaching his claim at mid-morning. The day had a crispness to it that she liked. It felt good to be out of town again and back on the river. Her high spirits fell when they reached his property.

Lily did not like the rough, windowless cabin Jack inhabited. If this was how the men lived when they were not in the bars, it was no wonder they were willing to throw bags of gold at her.

Next he took her to his digging site and together they entered the tunnel he had somehow carved from the permanently frozen ground. She knew from listening to the miners that only the top few inches ever thawed this far north. So the ground had to be melted by setting fires, waiting for them to burn down and then scraping off a few inches of thawed gravel before beginning the process again. Permafrost, they called it.

Jack's tunnel looked larger than the others she had seen from the river, large enough to use a wheelbarrow instead of a bucket to clear the material and high enough to stand in. Lily had feared she'd have to crawl.

"You must have been lighting fires day and night."

Jack smiled. "Not exactly."

He led her by lantern into his mine shaft.

"Is it safe?" she asked.

"The walls are frozen solid. See the ice?" He brought the light close to the side of the tunnel, pointing out the white crystals scattered through the gravel. "Can't collapse," he assured, pounding on the solid wall.

As they descended, Jack indicated different layers of sand and gravel, rock and strata, whatever that was. It all looked like dirt to her, but he seemed greatly excited by the tiny differences in color and consistency. He'd kept a record of how many dollars per pan he'd extracted from the various levels and the numbers kept going up as they went down. They were up to sixteen dollars a pan when they hit the end of his tunnel.

"How much farther down can you go?" she asked.

"All the way to bedrock and then I'll continue along, heading under the river. No matter where the gold came from or how long ago the ancient rivers deposited it, the placer gold can go no lower than bedrock. Might find some large nuggets down there."

Jack hung the lantern from a spike he'd driven into the wall of the tunnel. As he lifted the light she saw what he'd made out of the collection of metal and parts.

"Is it a steam engine?" she asked, stepping closer to touch the round boiler he had riveted together. *Impressive* did not begin to cover it. She'd seen the boat he'd made, but this was truly marvelous. "But why have it down here? And where are the wheels?"

Jack laughed. "No wheels. I place it, then fill it then use it."

"For digging?"

"That I still have to do."

"Well don't keep me guessing. What does it do, Jack?"

"It's a steam engine, as you said, but I use the steam to melt the ice and loosen the gravel. Then I only have to gather up the load and haul it up to my Long Tom and let the stream wash away the gravel."

Lily's eyes widened. "That's genius! All the mine owners will want one."

"I hope so. My next step is to gather investors and make more from this prototype. Then I'll sell the engine with instruction on how to use it to best effect." Jack waved his hands. "I patented it before leaving."

"You could sell them outright or take a percentage of all the mines that use your machine."

Jack cocked his head.

"That's a thought. But I'm still testing it. Perhaps, after I work out all the bugs. So you like it?"

She hugged him in answer, gratified to feel his strong arms wrap around her once more.

He didn't release her, so she smiled up at him, basking in the close familiarity of his embrace. His grin made him look boyish. She wanted to kiss him, but she reined herself in.

"I'm proud of you."

"Thanks, partner." He let her go and she had to stop herself from stepping back toward him as he moved to the machine.

"You'll make a fortune." Her smile faltered as she realized that the faster he succeeded in regaining his wealth, the more quickly he would leave her behind. The realization took all the joy from her. Her shoulders sagged.

"Come on." He drew out a match. "Let me show you how it works."

Lily spent the next hour waiting for the water to boil and then for the steam pressure to build, but once he had the engine up to heat, it melted the ice from the gravel like hot water through cold butter. Jack manned a rubber hose, fixed with a nozzle that helped him control the steam flowing from the end.

It was truly a wonder.

Jack extracted a wheelbarrow full of material in a matter of minutes, then released the steam and doused the fire in the boiler. He wheeled the material up to the surface and then sent it through his Long Tom, concentrating the gravel to just the heaviest matter, while the rest washed through the riffles and back into the river. She kept a sharp eye out for nuggets as he tossed away the larger pieces of waste rock.

After he had shoveled the last of the material into the box and let the water diverted from the stream wash over it, he slid a plank down across the top opening, shutting off the water. Lily helped him collect the sand and gravel that had survived the rush of water. The total barely filled his gold pan and she was disappointed to see no nuggets. He took the pan inside where he kept his washtub, right in the center of the ten-by-ten foot room. Nala appeared and then wandered out again, as he washed the concentrates free of sand. The gold seemed to grow before her eyes as the gravel fell into the catch basin. She plucked out the largest nugget, the size of an almond, and held it up toward the only light which streamed weakly through the open cabin door. The days were more and more overcast and she feared, though it was only September, that it might soon snow.

Jack extracted and measured the nuggets that were coarse and ranged from the size of a grain of rice to one as large as her thumbnail. When he finished weighing the haul, the single pan came to $2.50 worth of gold. Lily beamed with pride.

"Not folderol?" he asked.

She giggled and shook her head. "Seems I am wrong on some infrequent occasions."

His hands were wet, his face streaked with dirt and he still made butterflies quiver in her belly. She needed to touch him so she removed her handkerchief, using it to wipe away the grit from his cheek.

"If you'd have told me what it was, Jack, I'd have seen the point of it."

He captured her hand, staying it in midair. "Didn't trust you then."

"And now?"

"With my life."

He pressed his cheek to her hand, closing his eyes briefly as he rubbed his whiskered face over her palm, and then released her.

Why did he hold her and then set her aside? Was it because he still wanted her, but cared just enough not to use her when his intentions had not changed? That thought stole all the joy from his touch.

"Oh, Jack. It's not been the same without you. Why don't you come to my shows?"

He stared in silence as she waited, hoping to hear what it was that made him look so grieved.

"Once a week, Jack. It's only a few hours. Come for Saturday night. Do promise you'll come."

"I don't think that's wise." He hesitated, opened his mouth to speak and then clamped it shut again. Finally he spoke. "Is everything all right with you—since we parted?"

She nodded slowly, not understanding his odd expression, which looked like concern except for the tension in his jaw and the speculative lift of one brow.

"Never thought to find Dawson to my liking, but it's rugged and new, full of hope and promise. You needn't worry about me. I'm fit and flourishing. I love it here."

"But that's not what I meant. Is everything all right with you, since we..."

And suddenly she understood. Heat flooded her face and neck as she realized he was asking her if she was with child. So that was what this was about, his guilty conscience. She wasn't here to see his machine or give advice. That recognition hurt her more than his absence for she hated to be reduced to an obligation. No, she couldn't stand that.

She straightened, trying and failing to maintain a grip on her dignity. "You needn't worry on that account."

In fact, she'd had her monthly courses already, they'd come with a pang of regret that confused her. Had she really wanted to carry a child that he would see as nothing but an obstacle, an unwelcome tether to a woman he wanted to leave behind?

"There's nothing holding you here. When you're ready to go, I mean."

"I'm happy to hear it." But he didn't look happy, for he did not smile and his body remained taut with a palpable tension.

She turned away to stare out the door of his cabin to the yard where Nala gnawed on the end of a branch that was nearly as long as she was. How she wished she could love Jack as Nala did, without regret or shame.

Lily wanted to curl in a ball, wrap herself inward and rock like a child in her mother's arms.

She heard him approach, but could not bear to turn about. It hurt too much to look at him and see the remorse in his eyes.

Jack would hold her if she asked him to. He would comfort her and kiss her. He could take her up in those arms and she realized she'd let him, but she did not ask and he stopped before reaching her. She knew he still wanted her and she longed for him, but she had just enough pride not to ask and he had enough scruples not to use her as he had done.

Lily should be grateful, instead of resenting his restraint. She glanced back again, finding him standing, torn between his needs and his aspirations.

Well, she'd not make it easy for him.

"Take me back to town, Jack." She knew she had to go now or make an utter fool of herself.

She stepped out into the open air, glad for the chill that cooled her heated cheeks.

"Lily?" He rested a hand upon her shoulder.

She glanced back, then slipped from beneath his gentle restraint. "I'll be at the canoe with Nala." Lily patted her thigh and called to her dog. "Come on, girl."

Her hound left her stick and trotted along as Lily made her way down the bank.

Jack appeared a few moments later, holding the canoe as she climbed in. Nala leapt to the center and Jack pushed them clear of the bank. He paddled her home in silence.

After an eternity, he drew up to the riverbank in Dawson, but did not get out. Lily stepped ashore and Nala leapt clear with her, but Jack called the dog back. It was the first word he'd uttered.

She patted Nala. "Go on, girl."

Nala hopped back into the canoe's center section and whined.

Lily tried to keep the tears from betraying her, but was not certain she succeeded.

"Lily?" Jack's brows were lifted as if he did not know just what to make of her. At last he said, "I'll come see you on Saturday night." He waited and she made no reply. "If that's all right with you."

Which would be worse, seeing him or not seeing him? She nodded her consent and left him, hurrying up the grassy incline to the muddy road, away from the man who tore her insides up like glass through soft clay.

Chapter Fifteen

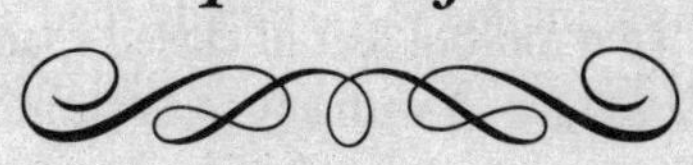

The following Saturday, Lily peeked through the curtain again, looking for Jack. She could not keep herself from checking every few minutes. As her music started and the curtain was pulled, he still was not there. The crowd erupted in cheers as Lily scanned the corners for sight of him, desperate as a castaway searching for land. She forced a smile and began her songs, performing the dance steps she had added, feeling low-down and blue. The audience did not seem to notice her false face as she held out hope until the very last number.

Still he didn't appear.

She called herself a fool as she gathered up her wrap and muff. But by slow degrees Lily's hurt feelings dissolved into concern until she couldn't shake the worry. He'd said he'd come and he hadn't. Jack might have done her a bad turn, but he'd kept his word on every occasion but this one. She knew she should go back to her room and go to bed, instead of contemplating a trip upstream in the middle of the night. But she found herself gathering up her sacks of gold and offering one to Bill Connor, a stagehand and bouncer. He had a lazy eye and wide shoulders, perfect for digging, but on reaching Dawson, he'd found he had a morbid fear of closed spaces and so was unable to hire on with any of the mining operations.

Bill was married to a pretty laundress named Babe, who Bill said made a fine living running her dirty water over a greased board to catch the gold dust that clung to their duds. Bill was smitten and Lily knew she'd not have to worry about any shenanigans when she was with him.

She held up one of the pouches of gold she'd collected from the stage. "This is yours if you take me downriver to Bonanza Creek."

Bill asked no questions, but pocketed the bag. "I've got to tell Babe. She'll be expecting me."

"Meet me at my place afterward."

He nodded.

"I'll walk you home, then go tell her."

Lily could not push down the feeling that something was wrong as they headed to Jack's claim. The timing was bad and they had to make their way in darkness, as the sun now disappeared for twelve hours and would not be up until after seven the next morning. The miners who had not come to town were all asleep, so Bill paddled undetected past the claims that lined the narrow creek.

Nala greeted Lily when she was still half a mile out. That she had wandered so far afield did nothing to ease Lily's growing concern.

Nala barked as Bill grounded the canoe and then hopped aboard before they continued on their way. Lily now urged Bill to greater speed as her worry turned to panic. It seemed to take hours to reach Jack's claim. At last the bottom scraped mud. Nala leapt from the boat, barking and cutting back and forth. The minute Lily had her feet, her dog was pushing her along. Lily did not need the urging. She lifted her skirts and ran.

"Jack!"

She arrived at his empty cabin, breathless and with a burning stitch in her side.

"Jack!"

She called again, to no avail. Nala barked from the mouth of the tunnel and then disappeared into the darkness. Lily's stomach dropped.

"Bring the lantern," she called to Bill.

Together they entered the tunnel, but as Lily continued, the light did not. She turned back.

"Bill?"

"I can't go down there, Lily. I'm sorry."

Why had she brought a man who was good for

nothing belowground? She dashed back to snatch the lantern from him.

"Wait here." Lily left him, hurrying into the cold earth, holding Nala's collar, pressing her fingers into the solid reassurance of her thick coat and warm skin. "Jack!"

Her voice echoed off the icy corridor. *Please let him be alive.*

Lily came to the steam engine and pressed a hand to the boiler. It was cold as the grave. Before her lay a pile of uncollected gravel. She fingered the dirt, finding it had not yet frozen solid. Hoisting the light she searched the ground, seeing the wall before her that marked the end of his work. Where was he, still back in town, at some other saloon or with some whore at the edge of town? Lily cursed herself for a fool.

"Jack?" she whispered.

Nala whined and began to dig as if in a rabbit hole. Lily stepped forward onto the pile of gravel. Something moved beneath her feet. Lily shrieked as she stumbled back. She lowered the lantern and saw that what she first thought to be a rock was Jack's boot heel.

Lily cried out, laying the lantern aside as she fell to her knees and began digging with Nala. After a moment she had exposed his leg. Her brain began to work now, the panic lifting.

"Find his head, you fool," she muttered.

Lily recovered the lantern and climbed the pile of debris. From here she could see that by some miracle his shoulders and head were not buried.

"Jack!" She ran to him, laying the lantern beside him and brushing back the gravel that covered his hair and neck.

"Lil?" he whispered. "Knew you'd come."

She stroked his cheek. "What have you done to yourself?"

"Pinned. Can't move."

Sweet Mother of God, was he paralyzed? Her heart hammered as she called her dog and together they dug.

"Bill! Get down here now!"

He didn't. She kept digging.

"Go to the next claim," she hollered. "Get help. There's a man buried here."

"I'm going!" came the reply.

Lily dug with her bare hands, scratching and clawing.

The digging caused more gravel from the top of the pile to slide into the place of what Lily had removed. Gradually she gained ground. She had part of Jack's back exposed when she heard the voices. Nala left her and a moment later two lights bobbed down the tunnel.

"What in the name of heaven?" said one, pausing at Jack's machine.

"Help me!" cried Lily.

They set to work with shovels and cleared the gravel from on top then hauled Jack roughly from his self-made tomb.

"Careful. He might have broken bones," said Lily, but they already had him up.

Jack's clothing and body were caked with mud and grime, but he was free. His eyes fluttered shut as he went limp between the two rescuers, who each held one arm about their own shoulders. Lily shrieked and wrapped her arms about his middle. He didn't rouse and his body was cold as ice, but the steady beat of his heart caused a wave of such relief she thought her own knees might give way.

"We need to get him out, ma'am."

Lily released Jack and followed the men up the tunnel. Jack's legs dragged along the ground. Lily broke out in a cold sweat, fearful he'd broken his spine. By the time they'd reached the mouth of the tunnel, his legs were working, but he still sagged heavily on his human crutches.

Lily now preceded the men, directing them into the cabin, where they lay Jack out on his bed. Lily took charge. "Bill, get a doctor. Don't come back without one." She pointed at the men. "Clean water, you." She pointed at the final man. "You, lift him up a bit, so I can strip him out of his clothing."

Jack groaned as she carefully peeled off the filthy attire. His skin was pale beneath his clothing and thankfully completely devoid of any blood, though his back and thighs showed large purple bruises. The first miner returned with a full pail, just as she finished wrapping Jack in her fur-lined cloak and his wool blanket.

"I need a good fire to heat the water and warm him. Does he have a pot?"

"He's got a gold pan," said the second. "That's what I use for washing and vittles."

Jack opened his eyes and smiled up at her, then winced. "Knew you'd come."

"Oh, Jack." The tears she'd contained spilled out.

"Saturday night then?"

She nodded. "Lie still, Jack. The doctor's coming."

Lily could barely breathe past the panic. What if his ribs were broken or he'd crushed something inside? What if he were bleeding inside right at this very moment? She swallowed hard as her vision blurred and tears splashed onto Jack's face.

His eyes opened. "Don't cry."

"I'm not." She dashed away the evidence and pressed her palm to his forehead. He was so dreadfully cold.

She glanced behind her to see the men both working over the stove, trying to get a fire started. Lily lay over Jack, pressing herself to him as she vigorously rubbed his arms.

After a few minutes his shivering began. The tremors were terrifying, spastic contractions that wracked him until he shook like a dead squirrel in the mouth of a hound. Throughout, Lily clung to him, waiting for the fire or for her skin to warm him. When the fire was good and hot, the men carried Jack to his only chair, setting him close to the heat.

Lily sat on an overturned bucket beside Jack to be sure he wasn't burned.

She heated water in a metal basin and when it steamed she added sugar and held it to his lips, tipping the cup as he drank thirstily.

His hands stopped shaking and he managed to hold the second cup himself.

"How long, Jack?"

"Ceiling came down Wednesday morning."

"Should have froze, I expect," said the first miner.

Jack looked up. "Hello, Nate. Likely would have, if Nala hadn't lain on top of me. Never left me." Lily recalled Nala coming to meet their canoe and wondered over it. Jack nodded at the other miner. "Daniel. Thanks for coming."

"What's that thing in your mine?" asked Nate.

"Something I'm working on," he said.

Lily's eyes narrowed on the man, her protective instinct engaging as she rose.

"He needs rest now. Thank you both." She hustled them back toward their claims.

"Call if you need us," said Daniel, doffing his hat. "You're even prettier close up, Miss Lily."

She gave him a smile and shooed him off, returning to Jack as quickly as possible. When they were gone, she hurried back to his side. He offered his hand and she clasped it, pressing his palm to her cheek. Her eyes drifted closed. He was here. He was safe and that was all that really mattered.

Lily stayed by his side, pouring hot coffee into him and keeping the fire going, until the doctor arrived. He checked Jack over and announced that his ribs were bruised, not broken and his body battered, but intact. The doc said the worst of his troubles came from lack of food and four days without water.

When he said that Jack should have died from dehydration, Lily cried again.

Before the man was even out the door, Lily was cooking. She made biscuits with gravy and Jack ate nearly a pan full. She helped him to bed and watched over him while he slept. When evening found him still sleeping, she crawled under the blanket and lay beside him. He roused enough to draw her into his arms, press his nose to her hair, inhale deeply, sigh and begin to snore for the first time. Lily felt herself relax. He would be all right. But what about the next time?

Chapter Sixteen

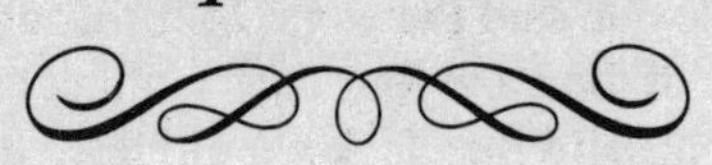

Jack woke to the aroma of frying bacon. For a moment he feared it was another hallucination, but when he opened his eyes he saw Lily by the stove in his little cabin.

It all came back to him in a rush: the collapse, realizing he was trapped and then Lily. Once again she was there when he needed her and she'd stayed through the night. He remembered waking long enough to weave a lovely thick strand of her hair through his fingers before dozing again.

"That smells like heaven," he said, trying to sit up and being momentarily arrested by the pain that shot through his ribs and down his back.

Lily was at his side in an instant.

"Are you aching? The doctor left some laudanum."

"That will just make me sleep again." Jack pushed himself to a sitting position, wincing despite his efforts not to do so.

"Coffee?" she asked.

He nodded, his head spinning with the pain of sitting up. Her arm was around him now, gently supporting him as she held the bitter and sweet coffee to his lips.

The heat filled his stomach and bolstered his spirits. Lily had not forsaken him. If she had treated him as he had her, would he have come? Her actions proved to him again how dauntless she was.

"Jack, what happened?"

"Stupid. I didn't consider the steam would not dissipate. It collected on the ceiling and then a section thawed. It all came down at once. The gravel hit me from behind, pinned my legs first and then my arms. When I came to, it had all frozen solid again, like a crypt. Just dumb luck it didn't suffocate me."

"It's too dangerous, the steam."

"No. It's not, but I learned something. The ceiling has to be braced until it has a chance to freeze up again."

"I don't want you going down there anymore. You can come live with me in town."

He frowned. Did she have so little faith in him? He'd learned a valuable lesson and knew the machine could be viable with just the addition of braces.

He shook his head. "I need to stay here and finish my testing."

"Testing? You were nearly killed, Jack. It's not worth your life, is it?"

He didn't answer.

"I promised to help you, Jack. You can stay with me until you're feeling better. No need to go back down in that tunnel."

"But I will go back."

Her eyes went wide and her expression fell. She started crying again and he wiped away the tears. It hurt like a son of a bitch to lift his arms, but he gritted his teeth and caressed her damp face.

"I was so frightened, Jack," she admitted. "I couldn't bear it if anything happened to you."

He rocked her gently back and forth, gritting his teeth against the ache in his ribs.

"Nothing happened. I'm all right now. When I got pinned down there, all I could think was that if I died your last memory would be of me hurting you again. Now, at least, I have a chance to ask your forgiveness."

She recalled him asking her if she was with child without coming right out and saying so. Lily could not bear to revisit that topic, so she gathered up his empty coffee cup and threw the dregs out in the open front door. Nala rose to investigate this new addition to her yard and Lily returned to Jack, perching on the edge of his bed.

"We made a mistake, Jack. Both of us. You don't have to worry about me. I understand the way things work and I'll land on my feet. Besides, I'm here for an adventure. I just got more than I expected, is all. Plus, if I were with child and needed a man to help raise it, I wouldn't have far to look, now would I? Dawson is crawling with candidates."

Jack made an involuntary growling sound. Did the idea of her foisting his child off on some stranger fill him with fury or just catch him off guard? She'd never seen such a black expression on the man.

His breathing increased and he went pale again. He fell back to the pillow, his eyes still fixed on her.

Lily studied Jack from beneath her lowered lashes. His frown and glowering expression pleased her far more than it should have. If any of her pretty speech were true she'd be past caring what he thought or felt for her. So why did she keep coming back to the well, knowing it was dry?

Jack forced himself up on one elbow, exhaling sharply as the pain took the color from his cheeks. "I don't want that."

She nodded her acknowledgment.

"And I didn't mean for it to happen."

She gave a mirthless laugh. "That's usually the way of it."

"I'd take responsibility for a child, Lily."

She pressed her lips together to keep from shouting that she didn't want to be a responsibility to him. She didn't want to be another obligation like his mother or his sister.

Instead she said, "I know, Jack."

He wasn't the sort to turn his back on her for he could have done that a hundred times along the journey.

His eyelids drooped.

She sighed. "Rest a bit."

She pressed a hand against his shoulder and he eased back into the narrow bed.

He closed his eyes, taking shallow breaths. Lily could not resist brushing the soft locks of hair from his forehead. He lifted his hand and captured hers, lacing their fingers, before rubbing her knuckle over his soft, dry lips. He kissed her there and then lowered their hands to the bedding as if the intimacy was nothing more than a brief thank-you.

But the soft caress and brush of his mouth made her stiffen as the rippling excitement gripped her insides and set off a shiver of hopeless longing. She stared down at him in hungry anticipation to find his eyes closed and his expression at peace.

Damn the man!

She tried to tug her hand free, but he resisted, holding her fast.

"Stay a little." He raised his lids as if bone-weary, looking up at her with his soulful whiskey-colored eyes, warm and welcoming as the autumn sun.

His eyes closed again. "Steamers are running.

That means there'll be goods. I can buy what I need to build more engines, just as soon as I scratch up the venture capital."

Lily wondered who would be fool enough to invest in a machine that caused cave-ins, but kept her doubts to herself.

"The steamers brought something else," said Lily. "A letter from my sister, Bridget. She gave me a rundown of all I've missed. They're struggling, of course, but all hale and healthy, thank the Lord."

"Younger sister?"

"They're all younger, remember, Jack? I hope they've received my letters. Won't they be surprised to hear what I've been up to?"

Jack grimaced as if ashamed of what they'd been up to.

"You needn't worry, Jack. I mentioned you only by your first name. Far as they know you're just another one of the men, out of work and desperate enough to come and try your luck."

He flushed and she knew she'd hit the nail on the head. Was it so humiliating to be associated with her?

"I didn't tell you not to mention me."

She pressed her lips together to keep from telling him that he didn't have to. His expression said it all.

Jack reached for her hand, there beside his on the bedding, but she lifted it and clasped hers together in her lap.

He changed course and lifted himself up, with a groan, leaning back against the wall behind his head. The pain squeezed through him and then was gone. He'd been lucky—very lucky.

"My sister, Cassie, will be ten in March. She should be in school now." A public school, he imagined. Quite a shock after attending a fine private school. She'd been on track to attend Wells College, like Mother, when their fortunes turned. "My mother's family owned a pharmacy in Rochester. It's how she met father. My grandfather wanted him to learn the ropes, so he sent him off on the road. When he brought mother home there was a row, but they came around. My mother is beautiful and accomplished and it wasn't as if she came from nothing. Her father owned his business, after all. The funny part was that *her* family did not approve of dad. Can you imagine? They wanted a professional man, not a salesman, and had no idea who he really was. Well, that turned the matter and my grandparents went to see Mother's parents. After that it was all smooth sailing."

He finished his story and smiled at her. His smile faded by slow degrees as he realized too late that he'd insulted her again. He cleared his throat and fell silent.

Lily picked at her fingernail, head lowered. "It's a pity you lost your pa, Jack. It's a hard thing."

He clenched his jaw. His father didn't deserve

Lily's concern. His father had abandoned them in every sense of the word, and Jack was tired of keeping up appearances.

That half-truth, told by instinct to protect the family name, now became intolerable. It didn't sit right to lie to Lily. He wanted her to know everything, even something this dark, for it was as much a part of him as his skin. So he straightened, preparing himself to tell her that his perfect little world was as cracked as an eggshell dropped on a stone floor.

"He wasn't lost, Lil."

Lily's eyes fixed on him, cautious now, for she knew him well enough to recognize his change in mood. Lily folded her arms protectively about her middle and lowered her chin before speaking. "He wasn't?"

"He left in the most cowardly way possible."

Jack wondered what she'd think after he told her. At home the news had spread like a breaking tidal wave, washing through the community. Jack had learned during that dark time that there was nothing so unforgivable as losing one's money, unless, perhaps, it was losing one's fortune and then putting a bullet in one's forehead.

In the end, the only visitors were the creditors who appeared with a speed of buzzards smelling a corpse.

"Jack?"

He lifted his chin from his chest and met her worried gaze.

"When my father learned we were ruined, that he'd lost everything, he...he killed himself, Lil."

She gasped, holding her hands over her mouth in shock, but he forged on, needing to get it all in before he watched her walk away like the others.

"He went into his study, used a revolver. I heard the shot and found his body."

Lily pressed her fists to her cheeks. "Oh, Jack, that's a terrible thing."

"Yes. Terrible." He looked up at her, holding her gaze. "Do you know what was worse? No one came to the house to pay their respects. Not one of my mother's close friends or a single member of any of the societies to which she belonged. It was as if we were contagious. I wonder if he knew what would happen, if he understood just what his actions would bring. He was a coward, taking the easy way out and leaving us to face the consequences."

He waited for her condemnation at speaking so frankly about his father or for her to remind him that his father burned in hell. She did neither. Instead, Lily slid her hand along the blanket until it rested on his.

"What about *your* friends?"

"I left school without telling them. Too ashamed to face them." He drew a breath, steadying himself to tell her the rest. "I was engaged back then, Lil.

She was the daughter of one of my father's business associates. I went to see her just after I returned from college to tell her the news. She cried, of course. So I tried to reassure her, comfort her. It wasn't until later that I realized she wasn't crying for me but for what *she* had lost. She waited until after the funeral to return the ring."

Lily blew out a long breath. After a moment she said, "She's a fool."

"She knew enough not to wed a penniless man."

Lily's smile seemed sad and wise all at once. "There's worse things. Like not having the decency to give your sympathies when a man has lost his father."

She was right again. He shouldn't care what they thought. He was lucky to learn so early just what kind of people they were. Unlike his poor mother who was still devastated by their swift rejection.

It was on her account, mainly, that he plotted his revenge.

"I still want to prove to them that my family doesn't need them. If I can make this work, my mother and sister won't have to suffer for something that was none of their doing."

"I would think there would still be talk."

"Don't fool yourself. Money is all that's needed for them to reenter society and those bastards will pretend that Mother was just in Newport for the season, instead of returning from exile."

The thirst for a triumphant homecoming still burned his throat. But now it was tempered by the knowledge that he didn't like them. He'd be well rid of the lot.

She squeezed his hand. "If you're needing to spit in their eye, Jack, well then, I'll help you all I can."

He should have expected it from her. She didn't turn her back on trouble, wouldn't judge him or think less of him for his need to set things right. Jack wondered if Lily had any idea how precious she was becoming to him.

Jack thought of his mother's telegram and frowned. When he'd come north, he had wanted to make good so they could reenter Society. He'd fought and struggled, determined not to give up. Now he didn't even know if he wanted to go back to New York. But he had to, because he'd not abandon his sister and mother as his father had done.

Now he dreamed of Lily at his side. But each time he tried to imagine her there, presiding over his household, overseeing dinner parties with business partners, he felt queasy. There must be a way to have her.

Chapter Seventeen

Lily stayed at his side while his body healed. Jack had been damned lucky. Cuts and bruises were all he had suffered. That evening Lily snuffed out the light and lay beside him, fully dressed, keeping him warm through the long night. He relished holding her, inhaling her sweet scent with each breath and snuggling safe and warm beneath the blankets.

He'd missed this intimacy.

Thursday morning he'd managed to get up on his own two feet and make it outside to relieve himself. The food and drink that Lily had been forcing down his throat had bolstered him more than he could have imagined, and he no longer seemed weak or confused. He had some spectacular bruises blossoming like purple roses on the backs of his legs and his torso. He guessed the fact that the collapse had been mostly loose gravel had saved him. Had there been a good-sized rock among the load he'd be dead, or worse—paralyzed.

By the afternoon he was well enough to sit at the table and share a meal. He loved playing house with her; Lily brought life even to this crowded, tiny cabin. No, he thought, she brought life back to him. He hadn't realized that part of him had died with his father. Jack had been so focused on his own mission that he'd had no time left to enjoy living. He'd built his machine and set it to use on his claim, working like a demon, going days without even seeing the sun rise or set. But all that had changed with Lily.

He knew she had to go back to town, but he wanted to keep her here. As he grew stronger and no longer needed her, he felt her restlessness and recognized she was preparing to go.

He knew he should let her.

Lily cleaned up after supper and poured the remains of the coffee into two battered tin cups. It had become their habit in the evenings to take turns washing up and then sit together by the stove with the last cup of coffee before bed. He coveted the time with her, talking about nothing and everything.

Lily went out first, leaving Jack with a gold pan full of warm water. The steam curled up into the dry air as he stripped and scrubbed himself with a rag and soap. He tried to ignore the hitch and tug of his stiff muscles as he forced them to move. Afterward he set his union suit aside, opting for only his jeans and soft blue flannel shirt.

Lily returned and he stepped out into the night.

The nights were growing longer now but the sun only receded for six hours, dropping from sight and then reemerging in the Northeastern sky.

He finished his business and retraced his steps, returning to her.

She handed him the wash basin, smelling of soap, her cheeks glowing bright from scrubbing. He tossed it out in the yard and entered, finding Lily now in the chair near the stove.

"It's getting darker again. Soon we'll be able to see the Northern Lights again," she said.

Jack nodded and then added more logs to the fire, in preparation for the night.

"We don't have anything like that back home. Can you see the lights in New York?"

"No, but I understand they do see them on occasion in the Adirondacks."

"I love them. I love everything here, and I've decided to stay."

He paused, crouching beside her. Did she mean here in his cabin? His heart accelerated at the thought of having her here.

"After all, what better life could I hope for? There are so many opportunities in the north for me and the land is so beautiful. I've never seen a prettier place on earth than here in Dawson. And I love the people. They're from everywhere and all with the same desire to make something for themselves and their kin. Self-made men—it's thrilling."

Jack frowned. He didn't like that plan; it would separate them. He stared at her bright smile and the vitality twinkling in her eyes. Why did she have to be Irish? Why couldn't he stay?

He hedged. "It's an interesting place. Likely change when the gold runs out, though. Might not be so easy to make a living."

Lily nodded. "I don't need much and there'll still be trappers and the lumber is good while it lasts. I just wish I could make everything stop and be the way it is right now."

Jack nodded and then retrieved his cup, not wanting to say anything that might break the quiet harmony.

"I think I'll be heading back to town tomorrow," she said.

Jack winced. Of course, her job was there and she was doing well with her singing. If his machine paid off and he could provide for everything she'd ever need, would she move in with him? His stomach knotted as he stared at her, wondering how to broach the subject that plagued him.

As silence stretched, Lily's eyes grew worried. "I'll stay if you need me."

He did need her, but not in the way she meant.

It wasn't right to keep her here now that he could get by without help.

"I can manage."

She dropped her gaze and nodded. Had he said the wrong thing?

"All right, then," she said.

"I'll take you tomorrow."

"You don't need to."

"I need supplies and I've got to see about investors, then get about building my engines. Sooner is better for me."

She held her cup in her hands, not looking at him as she spoke. "Well, if you think you're strong enough."

"I'm strong enough."

Lily stilled at that, the cup poised halfway to her lips. She lowered the coffee as she wondered if he had meant to imply what she thought.

She pushed the cup across the rough-hewn table as her desire for him gurgled up from inside. *Don't you do it, Lily.*

But she knew she would, knew from the intent possession of his gaze and the slow steady pulse down low in her body.

She'd do it again and consequences be damned.

Jack held his breath as she sat still as ice waiting for the kiss of the sun. When she lifted her gaze he saw the desire flash, but she remained motionless, her fists flanking her coffee, her knuckles white from clenching the cup. He watched the battle between body and mind as she looked at his hands cradling his cup, his mouth and finally his eyes.

"You're black and blue from your shoulders to your knees."

That was her mind talking now. Her body spoke as well, her chest rising and falling with the increased speed of her breathing and the lovely flush of desire spreading up her neck and into her face. Her pupils dilated until they were dark circles ringed with brilliant blue.

He gave her a half grin. "Only on the one side. The other didn't get a scratch."

She captured her lower lip between her teeth and his breath caught. Now his fists were clenched as well. He could almost hear the debate in her mind. Should she come to him or not? He stared at her mouth and prayed.

At last she stood, crossed the room and set the lantern beside the bed. Then she turned to him.

"But you want me to stay?"

He nodded slowly, afraid to go to her. Like a hunter sighting a deer in a meadow, he made no quick movements.

"More than anything."

Her smile lit up her beautiful face. She'd come here and saved him, stayed to nurse him and here he was planning to be a cad by taking advantage of her the minute he was well enough. That was no way to repay her kindness.

But he didn't want to let her go. If he could just think of a way to have her, just find some means to make her stay, not just for the night, but forever.

"The night then," she said and snuffed the light.

Jack settled back upon the mattress, taking nothing for granted. She'd slept with him since his rescue and he'd done no more than hold her. But he was stronger now and his body pulsed with blood and desire. He prepared himself to resist her enticing fragrance, soft skin and warm body.

She lay half against him as she had the first two nights. The mattress was too small for them both to lie on their backs and so Lily had spent the first two nights on one side or the other. When she faced him, her arm went about his middle in a relaxed hold that felt just right. But when she turned away, she pressed her back against him. Even on that first night, the contact of his hip with her soft, round fanny was a nearly irresistible temptation.

He lay still and stiff as a chunk of wood, waiting for Lily to settle. Listening for the soft breathing that would tell him she slept.

Instead, he felt her fingers unbuttoning his shirt.

"Oh, thank God," he breathed as he took her in his arms and kissed her. She accepted him, letting him explore her sweet mouth before pulling away. Next came the soft rustling of fabric and in a moment she was beside him, naked, her skin already beginning to grow chilled.

Jack stripped out of his clothing and slid in beside her.

"I've been dreaming of this every night," he growled, drawing her in.

Her throaty laugh was arousing as hell.

"I've missed you, too, Jack."

Tomorrow she'd leave him again, but tonight she was all his.

He held one hand on the center of her back, guiding her until she came to rest on top of him, stretched out from his chin to his ankle.

Lily settled her hips against him and made a sound of satisfaction in her throat as the soft curve of her belly pressed to his erection.

He leaned close and whispered in her ear. "You're driving me mad."

With exquisite slowness she trailed one finger over his chest and down his belly.

"Do you remember the first time I touched you?"

He did—that first day he'd arrived in Dyea, wet, cold, after Lily had rescued his dreams with his gear. He nodded, his chin brushing the top of her head. Lily's finger continued its maddeningly slow descent from his chest.

"You asked me why I did it. And the answer is, because I can't bear not to."

Chapter Eighteen

Her finger continued its torturous descent down his abdomen sending flames of desire licking down his belly to his groin. His hand stole up the warm velvet of her thigh.

She used her toes to shift her body upward until her lips were beside his head and her tongue caressed his ear. Jack groaned in delight.

He breathed in the spicy scent of her as she shifted to his side, giving herself access to all of him. Her fingers played along his skin, stroking his belly, teasing the fine hairs and following them south. He gritted his teeth at the sweet torture she wrought. Her hand moved to the base of his erection and his breath caught. He longed for her to wrap her fingers tight about his shaft.

But she did not grip him. Instead she used her

thumb to run the length of him, making his whole body twitch and jerk with the small spasms of delight.

"Do you like that?" she asked.

"Heaven," he breathed.

"And this?" Her fingers danced over his swollen flesh without mercy, arousing him even more.

His need grew large as the appetite of a grizzly waking from hibernation. He was insatiable, needing to feast only on her.

If he didn't stop her, he'd come right here in her hand. He grasped her wrist and lifted her fingers, taking each one into his mouth in turn and sucking the throaty morsels. He was rewarded with a series of tiny moans. In her delight, she arched toward him. It was too much to resist and he moved from her fingers to her throat, rolling her to her back so he could suckle the nipples of her lovely full breasts. He lapped and lathed one as he gently kneaded the other. She gasped and rubbed herself against him, offering what he most desired by pressing her nipple to his lips. He took the tiny bud into his mouth, using his teeth to tease the tender flesh. Lily bucked her hips.

He clasped her taut bottom and tugged her forward, lifting one leg to his waist. Then he slid his hand to her cleft, finding her slippery and hot with need.

He rubbed his thumb over her swollen nub of flesh and she shivered and gasped, tiny whimpers of delight encouraging him. His thumb continued to stroke and rub, exploring her body. She rolled to her back as he came to his side, grasping her leg and tugging her beneath him. Her hips moved in a rocking invitation against his hand.

Blood engorged him. He forced one leg between hers, bringing his knee up to the juncture of her legs. She moaned and lifted herself to rub against him.

Oh, sweet mother of mercy, he could wait no longer.

He moved into place above her and she spread her legs wide as he entered, lifting her hips to meet his. He stilled then, savoring the sweetness of this joining, wanting it to last all night. But Lily bucked, bringing him deeper into her body as her fingers raked his back, urging him on. The twinge of pain did not stop him but instead added to his pleasure.

He dropped one hand on each side of her head, holding his weight off her as he prepared to ride her as fast and as hard as she wanted.

With each stroke he sank farther into her sweet flesh. Lily threw her head back and her hands fell away, gripping each of his wrists for support as she writhed against him. Familiar cries told him she was close as she lifted and opened to savor each thrust. He gritted his teeth, trying to last, praying she would reach her pleasure before he found his. The race would be a close one. He'd never known a woman so full of life and so eager to take her pleasure.

It thrilled him and excited him far too much. He felt the battle lost as the sweeping surge of pleasure started deep within him. He plunged, arching as he pressed fully into her, his body quivering inside hers.

She cried out as he came in a hot rush of pleasure. And then he felt it, the rippling, rolling contractions of Lily's orgasm, squeezing him, pulsing about him, prolonging his own pleasure as he enjoyed hers.

So sweet.

If he lived a hundred years, he knew that nothing would ever be as good as this. What they shared was special. He knew it.

No New York socialite would ever hold a candle to Lily's passion, her beauty, her heart. It seemed suddenly very obvious that it was he who did not deserve her and not the other way around.

Reluctantly he shifted his weight from her, so as to allow her to breathe. She made a growling sound of disapproval in her throat and clung to him as he rolled to his back. He stroked her hair and wondered what he had ever done in his life to deserve spending even one night with her.

Lily startled and blinked. She lay half on Jack's chest wrapped around him like a monkey. How could she have fallen asleep like this? And then she remembered and blushed. She knew better than to do such a thing again, and yet, when she'd realized he was well enough to lie with her, she could not resist him.

She had considered for only a moment and dismissed all consequences and the realities of their situations.

No, those were best faced in the cold morning light. She blinked at the soft gray light that filtered through the cracks around the door. Her nose and cheeks tingled from the cold and she could see her breath. It seemed that the bedding and their bodies had kept them warm enough as the fire died.

She slipped from the bed, stifling a curse as the icy air attacked her from all sides. Lily hopped into her clothing with as much speed as possible and roused the fire. She glanced back at the temptation of the bed and Jack, but she knew what would happen if she ventured there again.

She gave a heavy sigh and headed out to find Nala. When she returned she found Jack dressed. He took her up in his arms and hugged her.

"Last night was wonderful," he whispered and then dropped a kiss upon her temple.

"Yes."

"Are you still going?" His breath heated her cheek and fanned down her neck.

She didn't want to. But if she stayed here she'd be no better than his… Lily nodded her head.

He pulled back and stared down at her with an expression she couldn't read. Disapproval? Regret? She wasn't sure.

"Shall I make breakfast?"

Jack stepped away, releasing her and taking up the coffeepot. "I can get something in town."

She nodded, feeling bereft that she had to leave this tiny little cabin and that he no longer needed her. Even if she stayed, it would change nothing; sooner or later he would leave, while she had decided to stay in the Yukon. There was no better place for the likes of her. Here she had a chance to be judged on her merit instead of her accent.

Jack set his cabin to rights and collected some of his belongings, including a nice cache of gold to take to the bank. A few more like that and he'd be on his way down river, she thought glumly.

Lily tied her cloak beneath her chin and raised the hood. "I'll wait by the water."

He nodded. As she walked away she could hear him muttering. Jack appeared a few minutes later, joining her and her hound in the canoe, and pushed off, pointing them downstream toward the sawboard metropolis of Dawson City.

Once in town she walked him to the bank and waited while he made his deposit. The bags of dust were guarded by Mounties who would escort the gold to the steamers that carried it to San Francisco. Jack's gold was in very good hands.

He let her pick the place for lunch and ordered eggs for them both as if they were not selling for eighteen dollars a dozen.

When she protested, he waved off her concerns.

"Have you ever thought of visiting New York, Lily?" he asked.

The rush of hope hit her with unexpected force, constricting her throat. But his guarded expression and furrowed brow made her pause, as she tried to understand what, exactly, he was proposing.

She tried not to let herself hope that things had changed between them, for she knew that no matter how much money Jack made, it would not be enough to gain her entry into society. So why did she hold her breath?

"There's nothing for me there," she said.

"I'd be there."

She cocked her head, confused by this sudden turnabout.

When Jack flushed and dropped his gaze, Lily's stomach flipped. What was he asking her that made it impossible to meet her eyes? She stared at him in confusion, for she would have imagined that New York would be the very last place on earth that he would wish to be seen with her…unless.

She set her shoulders as if readying herself to take a blow. "Say it plain, Jack."

"Always taking the direct route, up the trail, down those rapids and now here. All right, then. I'll say it plain." Jack rubbed his cheeks with both hands as he did when preparing to launch into something new. "Would you come with me, Lily?"

She bit her lower lip to keep from interrupting him

by shouting yes, held back by the dark suspicion that reared its ugly little head.

"If I sell my machines and I do well, I'm sure I could afford to buy you a town house. Somewhere fashionable. Twelfth Street even, only two blocks from Union Square."

"Buy me a..." The confusion cleared as her suspicion solidified like mortar, understanding now exactly what he was offering. He'd have to buy her a house, because she couldn't live in his. Not when he married another woman.

She stood, clutching her napkin in her fist as flames lapped at her face. "Jack, are you proposing to make me your mistress?"

He flushed as he glanced about at the other diners who had ceased eating in favor of taking in the free entertainment they provided.

He stood opposite her, reaching out to clasp her elbow. "Lily, please."

She twisted away, avoiding his grasp.

The waitress, who was scrawny as a stray cat, arrived carrying their plates, oblivious to the excitement.

"Eggs over easy?" she asked.

Lily never took her eyes off Jack as she spoke. "Give mine to the dog."

Lily's departure marked the beginning of a dreadful week for Jack. She would not see him, except from the stage and her friend Bill kept him from venturing any closer. She was clearly livid with him, and the more he thought about it, the more he came to the conclusion that she was right. He'd been out of line to ask her, especially when she'd only just finished telling him that she loved it here. What business did he have dragging her to New York and shutting her up in what amounted to an elegant cage? Lily needed to be free, to live a life of excitement, as her mother had wanted, not to exist in a half life as his mistress.

To make matters worse, word had spread about his cave-in and, as a result, he had no success getting potential investors to even consider laying down their hard-won capital on his invention.

He feared his only option was to mine his claim, take what he could manage to extract and then make his way home, tail between his legs. The thought of leaving Lily troubled him more than the recognition that he had failed. How was that possible?

He was sitting alone, nursing a beer at a dirty table in the Blue Wolf, a small saloon which sat on the corner of Harper and Third, when someone took the opposite seat.

He glanced up to find Lily staring at him with those intense blue eyes.

"No luck with the investors, I see."

His shoulders sank under the weight of his failure. Word had reached her of his failings. It reminded him of how he'd felt back there, after his father had died and before he could find the money to leave.

"No."

"How much does it cost to make one of those things?"

"Two hundred and sixteen dollars in materials each."

"And how many were you wanting to make?"

"Six to ten to start."

Lily stood, reached into her purse and withdrew a sack. The weight of it when it contacted the table and the way it remained upright and immobile, told him exactly what lay within.

"There's two thousand, Jack. See if you can talk the supplier down sixteen dollars a piece for buying in volume."

He stared up at her, astonishment rendering him dumb. There was no doubting from her expression she was still furious with him, yet here she was, offering him what must amount to all she had in the world.

"Why?"

"Because I promised I'd help you all I could. Now take it and do what you came to do, so you can go back there and reclaim what you've lost."

Chapter Nineteen

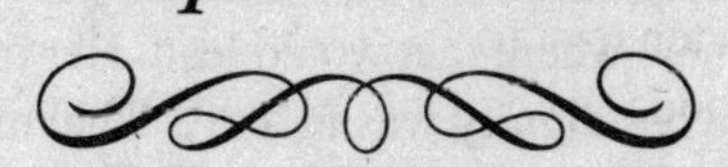

Lily called herself every kind of fool, for why else would she give him the means to pursue his dream instead of stamping it beneath her boot heel?

August had flown and September brought the first snow flurries. Since she'd handed over her fortune to Jack five weeks ago he had moved to town and now she faced the possibility of running into him on a daily basis. And though she knew she'd earn another bagful in the coming months, it didn't assuage the hurt. The night that had changed her life had not changed his.

When he'd asked her about New York she had actually thought she meant something more to him. Her own feelings for him had clouded her thinking to the point that she didn't understand that he meant to set her up in some shoddy room as his mistress.

Had he heard anything she'd said about what she wanted, about how much she loved it here?

Lily burned with shame at not being the kind of woman he could be proud of.

Word was that he'd managed to construct several machines and convinced some of the larger outfits to try them out. That meant Jack would be here through the fall and winter.

Lily knew where that would lead. Her only hope to salvage her dignity was to leave. That meant she needed to make enough gold to carry herself safely away, and to that intention she dedicated herself.

Word from the new arrivals was that the next big strike had been made by three lucky Swedes. Rumor was that gold was washing up on the beaches in Nome and although she didn't believe such talk, the men who had failed to secure a claim did and they were leaving in droves. Nome was over a thousand miles down the Yukon River. But now that the river flowed, ferries came and went with regularity, carrying goods and passengers, and would do so until the freeze-up, after which only the dogsleds used the river as frozen highway. It was best for her to follow them and quickly, before the need to be with Jack overcame her last shred of dignity.

Jack's business was well under way. By early October he'd built eleven machines and sold four already. They were up and running in the mines and the initial reports were so favorable he had appointments with three other mine owners.

As part of each agreement, he trained the operators in the use of the engine and taught them precautions so as not to be scalded by the steam. The contract stipulated bracing the ceilings, for he did not want a repeat of his accident. He believed firmly that his own mishap was the reason that it had taken so long to get his operation rolling. Word had spread that his machine caused cave-ins and that was bad for business. But now the results spoke for themselves.

Business was good. It was his personal life that was a tangle. He'd received four more letters from his mother begging him to come home. She was certain they could find a likely match if he were willing to look in circles outside New York.

Jack found himself making opportunities to run into Lily on the street. She always reacted in the same way. Her eyes went wide and then she plastered a false smile upon her face that would have done the women back home proud. She'd ask about his health or the business, but before he could tell her anything she'd excuse herself for some appointment or another.

He was a fool and he knew it. But he didn't know how to fix it. He hadn't meant to insult her, had only been trying to find a way for them. But Lily was a proud woman and it pained him that he'd hurt her so deeply.

Jack left town for his appointment craning his neck as he always did for a glimpse of Lily. He did not see her as he headed up the Eldorado to Claim #16, owned and operated by Fred Anderson.

The day was cold and cloudy, the tiny ice crystals stinging his cheek as he reached Anderson's mine earlier than expected. He found the miners working the end of an overnight shift. The foreman was covered in grime except for a band across his broad forehead where his hat must have been.

"Oh, so you're the inventor. Nice to meet you. We're running four times our regular tonnage and now that we've got the second steamer up, it'll go even faster."

Jack frowned. "What second steamer?"

"The boss bought a boiler from Kentucky Jim and rigged a nozzle—a bigger one—from a fire hose and he ordered another boiler that will arrive before the freeze-up. That'll give us three."

Jack felt a prickling unease crawling up his neck like an army of ants.

"You've braced the ceiling?"

"Yup. From the nozzle to a good twenty feet back."

"That's not enough!"

Next thing he knew he was running with the foreman at his heels. He reached the first group of miners on the steamer he'd constructed, but they couldn't hear him shouting over the sound of the nozzle blasting the gravel. The air was so wet it scared Jack to the core. He glanced up and saw only the operator stood under the bracing he had insisted run the length of the mineshafts. Jack turned a lever, releasing the steam. All the men turned toward him.

"Out!" he cried, grabbing one man after another and shoving them toward the main tunnel.

They stumbled back into the main shaft and stared at him as if he'd lost his mind. But when the crew foreman recognized Jack, he ordered them out and the men scrambled up the shaft toward safety as he reached the operator and sent him up as well.

"How many more?" he called to the fleeing man.

"Nine down below," he called back, still scrambling toward the surface.

Jack grabbed the lantern and headed down the main shaft. He could hear the other engine farther down. He lifted the lantern and looked at the ceiling, noting that water dripped from the passage. This was bad—really bad.

He reached the men, standing below the braced portion of the tunnel and turned off the steam.

"You're weakening the ceiling. Out! Everybody out!"

The men did as he ordered, but the tunnel was wide enough for only one at a time. Jack watched the lights retreating with the men as he waited his turn to flee. There was no sound with the first collapse, just a light that was there and then gone. Three more lights winked out as the men closest to him turned and ran back. He could see the lanterns bobbing before their terrified faces as they ran hunched over. There was a horrible scream cut short as more of the ceiling broke loose.

Only three men made it to the braced location to join him and the operator of the nozzle. Four of the nine now stood with Jack in the shelter of the timbers.

The men dug frantically through the loose gravel. The first man they unearthed was already dead. They dug no farther.

"They're all gone," cried one miner.

"Calvin was first. He might have made it out," said another.

"I saw him fall," said the last. "He's dead."

The first miner began to weep.

"Douse the fire in the boiler," ordered Jack.

"But it's light," argued the second.

"The fire will eat up all our oxygen."

One of the men snatched up the cask of water. Jack grabbed his arm.

"No. We may need that. Just scatter the coals on the ground."

They did. The embers glowed an eerie orange. Two lanterns remained. They doused one and turned the wick low on the other.

"They'll start digging us out as soon as the tunnel is safe," assured Jack.

But how much of the steam-soaked tunnel had come down? Would help reach them before their air ran out?

Lily dressed, stopped at the bank and then headed for the steamer offices. She had finally earned a tidy amount, enough to carry her to Nome and allow her to set up in a new boomtown. The threatening skies gave her the push she needed and by the time she reached the docks it was snowing in earnest. She watched the flakes vanish into the river. Soon it would be ice once more, the steamers would cease and the only way out would be by dog team—and Jack had her dog.

She picked a steamer leaving on Friday. That gave her six days to get her affairs in order and to retrieve Nala. Lily poured gold from her pouch into the scales to the correct measure and bought a one-way ticket to Nome. As soon as she lifted the ticket she felt ill at the thought of leaving Jack.

She headed up Front Street clutching her ticket with grim determination, knowing that Nala was just the excuse she needed to see him. If she thought about the reality of never seeing Jack again she'd lose her nerve. She was just going to get her dog. She put one more foot before the other.

"You're a fool over that man, Lily, and he'll be your ruination."

"Miss Lily?"

Had she spoken aloud? She turned to see Amos Luritz, the tailor, standing before her.

"Good morning," she said.

"Miss Lily, wait until you hear. Such news, I have. My business is so good, mending and sewing all day that I can't keep up. I had to hire an assistant!" he said, beaming. "Such a blessing and who would have guessed my fortune is coming from thread instead of gold? And it's all because of you. You gave me a business here."

"No, no. It's because you work hard and you are a very good tailor."

"Come spring I'll have enough to buy a ticket down the Yukon on one of these fine ferries. Sure will beat walking all the way from Dyea. And in Seattle, I'll find a steamer to take me all the way home to New York." His smile changed into a look of surprise when he noticed that she held a ferry ticket in her hand. "Are you leaving, too, Miss Lily?"

"I might be." No, she was. Why did she say *might?*

"What about your singing? What about your partner, the inventor?"

Was she really ready to sail to a new camp without him?

Lily squeezed the ticket, indecision twisting her insides. She should go, but she longed to stay.

"Mr. Luritz, I won this at cards and the company won't exchange it for cash. It's only to Nome and it leaves on Friday. Would you like it?"

She held out the ticket.

"No, no, Miss Lily, you've given me too much already."

She smiled. "But what about your beautiful daughters? Are you really going to spend another winter without them?"

He hesitated, eyeing the ticket. "I can't take it."

"You'll be home by Christmas."

He accepted the gift.

"Chanukah," he corrected. "Would you like to see their pictures now?"

Lily nodded. "Yes, I would."

He took a creased studio portrait from his pocket and extended it. Lily looked at the bright-eyed daughters surrounding a smiling woman and knew that she wanted to be as happy as this tailor's wife. She wanted it with Jack.

"You need to get home to them," she whispered, her throat now constricted.

He nodded, taking the picture and looking down, brushing a finger over his wife's face. "I do." When he looked up his eyes were swimming in tears. "How can I thank you?"

"By getting back to your children, of course."

The shouting in the street brought both Lily and the tailor about.

A red-faced man with a sunken stomach and a full mustache shouted again.

"Cave-in!"

Lily's heart stopped. Where was Jack? Her knees went to water and the tailor caught her before she hit the boardwalk. Terrible possibilities arrested her, making it hard to breathe.

"Miss Lily?"

"Where?" she whispered.

"Anderson's claim," shouted the stampeder. "All men to the site for digging."

She found she could breathe again, until she remembered that Anderson was using Jack's invention.

She headed out with the others.

She was nearly to the claim when Nala greeted her. Jack was here.

Lily sank to her knees, hugged her dog and prayed.

"Please, heavenly Father, let him be aboveground."

But he wasn't. The information was confusing and she had to speak to many men to learn that fifteen had been down in the mine on two steam engines. Jack had cleared six from the first machine and was heading to the next when the shaft gave way.

Lily found one of the survivors, a pale Welshman named Bobby Durham. A dirty, lopsided black hat sat low over his eyes that darted about in a frantic sort of way. He was smeared with mud and still shaking.

"Where's Jack Snow?" she asked.

"Dunno."

"You were with the second crew?"

He nodded, wiping the sweat from his face and smearing the mud onto his cheek. "I'd be dead if not for him. Brian was right behind me. Then the others."

"Where's Brian, then?" she asked.

He put his head in his hands and wept.

Lily clasped his shoulder.

Durham began a steady rocking to accompany his sobs.

"The others?" she demanded.

His voice was muffled by his hands pressed over his mouth, but she made it out.

"Behind me when the ceiling fell." He looked at her, his eyes crazed with grief. "The whole thing slipped loose and fell."

"Wasn't the tunnel braced?"

"Over the engine."

Lily's stomach churned as she realized what might have happened. She swept the area for Anderson. She found him, ordering men about.

"Mr. Anderson."

He turned to her, his face registering surprise at finding her here. "Miss Lily!"

"Was the tunnel braced?"

"I got no time for this now."

"Jack told me that the entire tunnel had to be braced so the steam wouldn't weaken the earth."

Anderson looked around at the men who had gone still and silent.

"He never said so."

Now she understood. Wood was expensive and Anderson had not done as he was told. Jack had come to check on operations, found the oversight and ordered the miners out. Her eyes narrowed on him, but she reined in her fury. This was not the time.

"How many men are trapped in there?"

Anderson cleared his throat. "Nine unaccounted for."

"And Jack?"

Anderson motioned with his head. "Among them."

Durham was on his feet now and facing Anderson. "He came to warn us. Told us to get out. Saved my life." Durham stepped up to Anderson. "You knew?"

Obviously, the miner had figured out who was responsible, and much as Lily would have liked to let Durham strike Anderson, she needed information.

"Was any of it braced?"

Anderson nodded. "Yes, over the engines, where the ceiling is wettest. I never knew that this could happen. I swear to God."

Lily knew it was a lie. Soon the others would know as well, for though she had not spoken to Jack, she'd heard from her regular customers who worked for grubstakes that Jack came to the mines to teach them how to use the engine. But she'd gain nothing by arguing.

Four or more hours had passed and they had achieved nothing. How much air would there be in the small chamber in the frozen earth? Had any of them even reached the braced portion?

Lily went to the mine entrance, now buzzing with men hauling out dirt in a bucket brigade. The buckets traveled hand to hand like a centipede moving its legs. Lily stared at the pile of earth they had moved and tried not to let the tiny flame of hope within her die.

She sat helpless beside Nala as the pile of earth grew. Shouts came from inside the tunnel.

"They found a body," came the call repeated from one to the next.

Lily's heart stopped as she waited. Another hour passed before the earth released the man. Durham's partner, Brian, just two yards back of him, was carried out on a plank. Dirt clung to his clothing. Someone had covered his face with a red handkerchief. But the bruising on his hands and the unnatural concavity of his chest deformed the corpse. Lily held her breath at the horror while the procession passed before her.

Durham howled like a frightened child as his friend was laid on the cold ground. Lily knelt beside him and prayed for the Lord to save the man she loved.

She sat back on her heels as the realization settled over her like a shroud. She loved Jack and she might never get the chance to tell him. What if she had lost him for good?

Grief, black as poison, welled within her. Inside, she screamed out her pain and horror. Outwardly, she could not even lift her hand to wipe her face.

Durham had recovered himself somewhat and swept an arm about her.

She turned to him. "Jack's gone, isn't he?"

He blinked at her, his eyes red-rimmed and watery.

"He was shouting and pushing us. Last I saw him he was headed deeper to the second team."

Lily pressed her hands to her face and sobbed.

The miner continued. "But that means he was well back and closest to the section they braced. He might have made it under the timbers before all hell broke loose."

Lily lifted her head. Jack would have placed himself behind the others as he ushered them out and that act of heroism might just have saved him from the falling rock. They needed to get to him quickly.

She clasped Durham's forearm. "How long would the air last?"

The weary miner pushed his dirty fingers beneath the crown of his hat and scratched his head. "I don't rightly know."

Dark came early now and the icy snowfall added to the misery. The men in the bucket brigade stood, cold and wet, passing the gravel from one to the next as twilight closed in and lanterns were set every few feet along the line.

It was full dark when they dragged out the mangled body of Calvin Toddy. Hope flagged as the men acknowledged that the chances of saving anyone was dropping with the temperature. Anderson's men stayed, but some of the volunteers abandoned the line. Men who had come to the aid of the victims were not going to waste precious days and hours digging dead men from the earth, not when the breath of winter was already on them and the smallest streams showing thin coatings of ice at night.

The pace slowed as a skeleton crew continued grimly through the night, sure that their rescue mission had changed to one of recovery.

Lily stood in grim silence as a pall settled over them all. The black shroud of grief threatened to take her again. Even if the men had survived the collapse, she recognized now that they wouldn't reach them in time.

That meant she had seen Jack for the last time, heard the final utterance from his lips and received her last kiss.

What had she said to him on the street yesterday? She could not recall, but realized that she should have followed her heart and thrown herself into his arms, instead of cloaking herself in her foolish dignity. Now it was too late.

Chapter Twenty

Lily's ears rang as she stumbled along the path that led back toward Dawson. Someone clasped her elbow, supporting her, keeping her moving.

"No!" She dropped to her knees in the dirt.

Jack was back there. Alive or dead, he was there and she would stay until he was found.

Against the blackness that threatened to consume her, she fixed on the pinprick of light. Jack had been last in line to leave. He might be under a small section of the tunnel that had been braced…waiting in the darkness. At this second, he might still live.

Lily found her feet and retraced her steps.

She found Anderson sitting at the mine entrance, directing men to send the dirt from the bucket brigade through the Long Tom to extract any gold.

Lily fumed. He had the manpower to search for

gold but not to dig out his men. It took a moment to realize that the men on the line were no longer passing the buckets from hand to hand, but carrying them several yards each.

"Where are all the others?"

Anderson shifted the cigar to the opposite side of his mouth. "Gone, like you should be."

"But they may be alive."

Anderson said nothing to this. Instead he brushed off the snow that clung to his coat and shifted the soggy cigar from one side of his mouth to the other.

"I'm sorry, Miss Lily. Men aren't going to leave their own diggings to muck about after men that's clearly passed. Winter's coming. They got to get the gold out while the water's flowing."

Lily felt the darkness creeping stealthily forward, threatening to take her to that place where she could not fight again. She pushed against it. Jack needed her.

"We could hire more men."

"What about if you do the singing and I do the mining?"

It was all she could do not to point out his shortcomings to date.

"What if *I* paid for a team of miners to dig?"

He blew a frustrated breath past the cigar which had long ago gone out. "I'm already digging. Tunnel's only wide enough for one man. And I'll have them run twenty-four hours."

"I could tunnel alongside you or…" Lily paused as the idea sprang at her all at once. Could it work? "How deep is the tunnel?"

"Hit bedrock at eighteen feet and been tunneling along it for some time."

"Why don't we tunnel straight down from the top?"

Anderson sat back and thought. "It's less earth, but the chances of hitting the steam engine right dead on, well it's twenty to one."

"What are their chances if you go in the main tunnel?"

He'd run out of excuses and so just stared at her a moment.

"It's a waste of time and money," he said at last.

"But what if it's my time and my money?" she countered.

"The dirt you dig is mine."

She nodded her acceptance of his terms.

"I'll get you the wood to set the fires and thaw the ground, and, hell…" He rubbed his neck. "I'll need to hire new miners anyhow. Might as well do it sooner as later. You'll have a crew soon as I can raise one."

"Thank you."

He removed his cigar and fixed her with a steady stare. "Snow was a lucky man."

Jack closed his eyes and prayed that the other steam engine had not been crushed in the tunnel collapse, for they'd need it if there was any hope of moving all the earth between them and the outside. Then he prayed for the souls of the men he'd tried to send to safety, only to see them fall.

When he opened his eyes he noticed the lantern flame flickering. He knew the lantern ate their oxygen, but he could not bring himself to snuff it. Somehow to sit in icy darkness was too much to bear. The effort of digging or using the steam engine would burn up too much air. None of the men had a watch and time did funny things when there was no daylight. Had it been twenty-four hours or two days? He listened for the sound of digging, praying that help would come.

He needed to see her again, needed to tell Lily that he'd been a fool. How could he ever have thought of his partner as anything less than what she was—the object of his desire, the reason to go on living and the equal partner he did not deserve? He didn't need to return to New York, and it pained him that he had set himself such a vengeful ambition. The one person whose opinion really mattered and the only one who believed he could succeed was Lily.

If he lived, he'd tell her what a fool he was. He'd beg her forgiveness and pray she would take him back.

Lily looked out over the chaos of the rescue. The first steam engine had been recovered. But they had found no survivors. In twenty-four hours she had the wood hauled up the mountain to the digging site and erected tents for the workers to rest when they were not digging.

She had set up a kitchen on-site, brought in food and men to prepare it. But they had made only twelve feet in the first twenty-four hours. Now at the thirty-sixth hour they were down eighteen feet and had hit neither tunnel nor bedrock.

What if they missed the men by a few yards?

Anderson's first team continued to dig slowly through the collapsed tunnel, finding no more dead, although five men remained missing.

The shift ended and the workers, tired and dirty, lined up to be fed.

That afternoon the Mounties arrived to begin an investigation of the collapse. They interviewed Lily and several of the miners, while Lily chaffed at the delay.

The new foreman, Doug Donaldson, a thin man with a knobby nose and a knot on his forehead, came to her at the kitchen tent. The snow had changed to rain, hampering their efforts to burn the earth enough to melt the ever-present ice.

"Are the fires going out again?" she asked wearily. Her bones ached now from the tension. "I told you to build them under the cover of the roof of the shelter and just transfer them."

"Coals won't do no good. We've done struck bedrock."

Lily's stomach flipped. Had they missed the tunnel or was there was no tunnel to strike?

She rushed to the hole that more resembled a well than a mine shaft. Had they dug too far forward or too far back, a little right or a foot left? She didn't know.

From down below the clang of steel on rock reverberated through the soles of her boots.

Lily tried to think which way the tunnel had been. No, that wasn't right. She meant which way the tunnel *was.*

The tunnel lay on bedrock and the men were not above or below that. That left a full circle of choices to try. She had often thought, when creeping down an alley in San Francisco or a dark hallway in the tenements, that distances seemed longer in the blackness. With that slim knowledge base, she made her decision. The clanging ceased and from down below came the shout of one of the men.

"It's solid, Miss Lily," the digger cried. "Now what?"

"Dig back toward the tunnel entrance." She pointed, trying to force a calm confidence into her voice. "That way. We've just missed it."

A moment later she heard the sound of a pick striking frozen ground.

Lily thought of her mother and the last act of love

she had performed for her, preparing her body for burial, and she wondered how much longer she could pretend that she had some meaningful reason to continue, that there was a shred of hope.

Jack straightened. His chest rose and fell with rapid, increasingly useless breaths. The lantern flickered dangerously and he knew they were reaching the end. He couldn't tell if the light was dimming or if it was his vision.

"What was that?" croaked Henderson.

"A vibration. Did you feel it?" said McKinsky.

"I don't feel nothing."

The men sat still and silent in the darkness. Seconds ticked with the rapid beating of his starving heart. Then it came again.

"There!" cried Henderson.

"I felt it," whispered McKinsky.

"Coming from that way," said Jack, inching toward the front of the tunnel. "Grab your picks. Hit the bedrock so they know we're here."

Just as the men snatched up their tools, the lantern sputtered and snuffed out.

Lily sat at the opening of the hole, watching the bucket of dirt slowly rising from the earth on the pulley system the men had rigged. They might just as well be digging with a pair of tweezers for all the earth they moved. It was too far down to start a fire. By the time they set it and let it die out the shift would pass, so she had ordered them to use their picks.

Down below her in the hole the men stood to wipe their foreheads, stilling for the time it took to draw the damp handkerchief across their faces, and she resented the delay.

"Damn, I've a powerful thirst," said one. "Think she'd lower down some water?"

"Would you want the man digging you out to stop for water? No rest until the shift is done."

"What's that?" said the first.

"What's what?"

"That shaking in my feet."

They stilled, both worrying that the twenty feet of frozen earth might somehow break loose and bury them as well.

"Feel it?"

"Yeah, like someone tapping," whispered the other, and then let out a shout. "Miss Lily! There's somebody banging on the bedrock!"

Her head and shoulders appeared over the opening, placing her in silhouette, like an angel coming from heaven above.

"Which direction?" she shouted, excitement ringing in her voice.

The men put their ears to the frozen ground and listened. They shared a knowing look and one nodded.

"This way," said one.

"Then dig, boys! Dig like it was you trapped in that pit," she called.

The picks rang against the soil, chipping the frozen earth as if it were baked clay. A niche appeared and then a foothold and then a divot. The earth would not yield easily, but the men were strong and determined.

"Stop, stop!" shouted one. "Listen."

They did, but heard nothing in response.

"The tapping's stopped," they shouted in unison.

Lily lay on her belly, peering down.

"Then dig faster!"

They scrambled to do her bidding. The picks whistled and clanged and then came a hollow sound a moment before they punched a hole.

They thrust the lantern into the gap and peered inside.

One got his head and shoulders into the tunnel.

"They're not moving," he called. "I think they're dead!"

Chapter Twenty-One

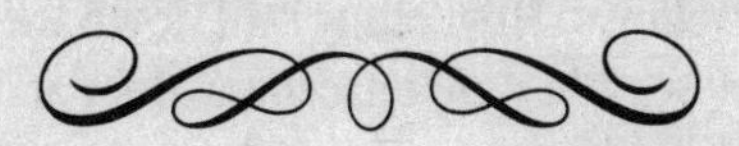

The words pierced Lily's heart like shards of broken glass. But Lily did not let her heart break, not yet. Not until she'd seen Jack herself. Instead she did what she always did when her back was to the wall—she fought. She shouted from her place at ground level, her voice now authoritative and shrill as any commanding officer.

"Don't think! Drag them out. Hurry!"

The miner reached a tentative hand forward and clasped the arm of the nearest man. He gave a groan.

"Alive! This one's alive."

Lily turned from the hole. "Get a rope and some men to haul these miners up."

The first body was yanked from the shaft dirty and still. She could not tell who the miner might be. She paced at ground level like a caged animal, waiting, praying as the man was hauled up.

He crested the rim.

"Dan Slater," cried one of the miners. He knelt beside the inert form. "Breathing."

They carried him to the tarp and laid him on a blanket, wetting his face with water on a rag. His eyes fluttered open.

"Am I dead, then?" he whispered.

Lily stroked his cheek. "Alive, Mr. Slater, as I pray are your fellows. How many still down there?"

She knew eight were unaccounted for and she held her breath for his answer.

"Four."

She tried not to let that crush her hopes.

"Their names?"

"Henderson, McKinsky, and the damned engineer who made that hell machine."

Lily left him in the care of the tailor, Amos Luritz, who had followed her to the mine and had refused to leave with the rest of them. She hurried back to the hole where another man was lifted, limp as a rag doll. This was Henderson, the operator of the engine, and he did not revive so quickly. In fact, he did not rouse at all, but his breathing was regular so Lily returned to her place. The next man crawled out on his own: McKinsky, his shoulders so broad he could barely fit through the opening. It took four men to haul him to the lip of the crater where he kicked and clawed his way back to the surface. When she looked back down she saw another still figure with the two diggers.

"Cummings," called one and motioned for the rope.

Where was Jack?

And then she saw him, crawling weakly from his prison.

"Snow," called the miner.

"Jack!" she cried, lying on her belly in the mud to be closer to him, reaching both hands down into the pit.

He lifted his dirty face and held a hand up as a visor as if the dim light from the cloudy day was too bright for him to see.

"Lily?"

They looped the rope beneath his arms.

"What are you doing here?"

One of the diggers slapped him on the shoulder. "She'll be real glad to see *you.*"

Jack's feet left the ground and he dangled between heaven and hell, ascending like an angel to the pearly gates. Lily was here. He blinked against the bright light that nearly blinded him after so much blackness. The last he remembered was the hammering and then…then he could not breathe and then, nothing.

He looked at Lily's sweet, stern face, staring at him as a mother would at a wayward child, happy at his return and angry that he'd ever left. He raised a hand in recognition at his fierce little partner.

How brilliant to dig straight down. They never would have reached them in time otherwise.

From below came the call. "That's all. Beyond this pocket, the tunnel's collapsed."

"Haul them up," Lily said to the men working the pulley system. "Take my hand, Jack," Lily said.

She grasped hold and would not let go, even as the men dragged him back to the surface. His legs gave way, but they pulled him back from the chasm. The sweet fresh air filled his lungs and snow melted on his cheek. What a miracle!

She fell to her knees beside him and he looked up into the face that he had longed to see.

He grinned at her. "Howdy, partner," he said.

"Oh, Jack!" Lily cried, and threw herself at him, clasping her two small arms around him and squeezing so tight that she pressed the very air from his lungs. "I thought I'd lost you forever. I thought…"

Was she crying? He drew back, holding her face between his hands.

"Lily, I'm all right now."

"I was afraid I'd never get a chance to tell you…to say…oh, Jack." She kissed him hard and then drew back to assure herself that he was really here in her arms.

He stared at her. "I must have died after all then."

She clung tighter. "Don't joke about that. Jack, I was wrong about everything. I love you, and all I want in the world is to be by your side. If you still want me to be your mistress, I'll go with you to New York or anywhere you say."

Jack stilled, but Lily clung, afraid that she'd lose him again, afraid that he'd changed his mind and no longer wanted her.

"You love me?" He stared, his expression so serious it frightened her.

She nodded.

Her eyes rounded and the lump in her throat seemed to grow. She could barely breathe past it.

"Please, Jack, say something."

"I was wrong about us, wrong to ask you to come with me."

Her heart, already battered as an old tin pail, now twisted in dread. After all this, had she lost him anyway?

She interrupted him before he forced her to go. "Please, Jack, give me a chance to prove how much I love you."

He stroked her cheek. "You already have, time and time again. But I don't want you to be my mistress, Lily. I'm ashamed I ever asked you."

Ashamed. Yes, it had been the trouble from the start.

"I understand, Jack. I know the way of it."

He placed his hands on hers, holding each one as if she were precious to him instead of an obligation he must discharge. Well, she'd not stand in his way. She loved him too much to be a shameful little secret or worse an open scandal. His thumb swept in circles over the back of her hands.

"I don't think you do."

How she would miss the deep rich timbre of his voice.

"When I was trapped, it was your face I saw and your voice I longed to hear again. I can't get on without you. I've fallen in love with you, Lily Delacy Shanahan, and I want us to be together—always."

"What?"

"I love you, too, Lily. Madly and with my whole heart."

Her head snapped up and she looked into his whiskey eyes as the shock of his words washed through her.

"Love me?" She gaped.

He nodded, one corner of his mouth quirking as he continued to hold her gaze. "Desperately."

The cresting wave of joy broke over her and then reality returned, stealing her elation. "But, oh, Jack, what should we do?" His family wouldn't accept her, his friends, his associates.

"Marry, I hope."

The astonishment of his proposal brought her scrambling in an effort to stand, but he held her.

"Lily, I love you and I don't want a mistress. I want a wife—I want *you* as my wife."

She was shaking her head madly from side to side. "But I'll ruin everything. You *can't* marry me."

"I can, if I can convince you to forgive me for my colossal arrogance and agree to accept me."

Lily's legs went rubbery and her head began to spin. The ringing in her ears made her own voice sound tinny and strange. "But what about New York, your mother and...everything?"

"Funny about that, I don't really think I belong there anymore. Not when everything I have come to love is here."

"What do you mean? You're not going back?"

He drew her into the shelter of his arms.

"I realized something down in that hole. I'm not the man I was when I came here. I feel sorry for those fools back there, jostling for social position and spending all they have to impress people they don't like to begin with. That's not for me anymore."

He stroked her cheek and she felt her heart stop. What was he talking about?

"You want to stay in the Yukon."

He nodded. "There's nothing I want or need that I can't find right here."

It was her fondest desire to remain in the northern territory, and to have Jack at her side would make the adventure so much sweeter.

"We could make a life here, Lil. You and me. What do you say?"

"I say yes!" She hugged him.

He cradled Lily against his strong body, leaning

her back, taking her lips with his in a kiss filled with love and promise.

Nala barked, startling them both. Lily drew back as her black Newfoundland licked Jack across the muddy dark stubble of his cheek.

Lily laughed. "I think she approves."

Jack grabbed Nala and hugged her, too. The three of them sat in the mud together and Lily thought she had never been so happy.

Jack made an attempt to stand, but swayed. Lily was there helping him as she had been from the start. He looped a hand about her shoulders and stretched, drawing a breath of air and then grinned down at her.

"We'll have a grand life, Lily, one full of adventure just like your mother wanted for you. And one that will make us both proud, because it will be ours."

"But Jack, what about your mother and sister?"

"We'll see they get what they need, help them all we can, just the same as we will your family. Soon as we get on our feet again."

"I'll help you, Jack."

He nodded, then swallowed, as if something blocked his throat. "Yes, I know you will, just as you always have. I should have seen that a long time ago. That day I met you on the beach was the luckiest of my life."

She patted his chest with her open hand. "You didn't think so at the time."

"Because I didn't understand then that you were the only partner for me."

"You're sure?"

"Yes, Lily. Partners forever and always."

Epilogue

One month after the collapse, Commissioner Ogilvie of the North-West Mounted Police completed his investigation, finding Jack blameless and commending him on the rescue of the miners. Anderson was cited and agreed to pay damages for the deaths at his claim.

The mine owners using Jack's engine were allowed to recommence operations and the general consensus was that the steam greatly aided the miners and was less dangerous than setting fires in the shafts.

Lily had left the stage to prepare for her wedding and on a cold November day she stood on a crate in the back of St. Mary's Church as Amos Luritz finished the hem of her wedding dress.

The tailor had missed the last ferry out to help

with the rescue. Lily meant to see he was aboard the first boat come spring.

She fussed with the scalloped lace trim at her throat, admiring the sheen of ivory satin bodice as Mr. Luritz finished attaching the last of the pearl buttons that lay straight as her spine.

A knock sounded at the door. "They're ready, Miss Lily."

"Yes, coming."

Amos bit the thread and stepped back, clasping his hands and smiling with delight.

"You remind me of my Tessa. Such a beauty. May you have all the happiness we've shared."

He offered his hand and Lily stepped down. "Thank you, Amos."

"You'll excuse me for being a nosy yenta, but who is walking you down the aisle?"

Lily lowered her head a moment, then gathered herself up, not wanting to spoil her happiness with even a moment's thought of the father who had never been there.

"I'm afraid I am walking alone."

"Well, I've never been in a church before, Miss Lily, but if you'd grant a man his wish, I'd be honored to escort you to your husband. Such a blessing."

Her heart twisted and she was afraid she might cry.

She extended her hand. "Oh, Amos, I'd be very grateful."

He lifted his elbow and she clasped it. When they reached the door she turned and snapped her fingers. Nala, sleeping beside the stove, startled awake, stretched and trotted to her side.

Mr. Luritz reached in his pocket, retrieving the remnant of lace and the tiny blue satin pillow which held two perfect golden rings cast from nuggets from Jack's claim.

He stooped and tied the lace about Nala's neck. "Such a ring bearer I've never seen."

Lily scratched behind her dog's velvety ears. "It wouldn't feel right not to have her here with us."

Amos patted Nala's wide black head and stood, opened the door and offered his elbow once more.

She nodded to Bat Samuelson, who cracked his knuckles and began to play a fast, upbeat version of "Ta-Ra-Ra Boom-De-Ay." The tinny chords drowned out the sound of ice hitting the windows behind her. It had been a struggle to get the piano across the street from the Forks with the ice and snow now freezing the ruts in place until the thaw, but Lily had managed it. Everyone stood and turned to look as she paused in the entrance. The assemblage, mostly men, removed their hats and pressed them to their best clothing, smiling at her.

"Go on, girl," Lily said to Nala.

Her dog glanced back and then preceded them, stopping only once to sniff one of the pews. Amos clasped Lily's hand at his elbow and lifted his chin, setting them in motion. As she began her journey down the aisle, the piano player switched to "Oh, Promise Me."

The miners, obviously unaccustomed to weddings, whistled and applauded as she passed. Two men even waved. She blew them a kiss.

The little church glowed with candlelight, shining bright as a new penny. Pine boughs tied with white ribbon decorated the altar before which the minister waited, Bible in hand.

There to her right, stood Jack. He wore a black suit and a gleaming white shirt, a thin black tie with a gold nugget tie tack big enough to choke a cat. His thick hair was combed, parted and slicked back; she imagined he might have looked like this back in that world he had left for her.

Amos took Lily's hand and placed it in Jack's.

"You be good to this one," he said. "She's got a golden heart."

Jack nodded and guided her to his side.

"Dearly beloved," began the priest.

Lily knew that she would remember this day for the rest of her life.

"May I have the rings?" asked the priest.

"Nala," said Lily.

Her dog stood still and elegant as a greyhound as the priest untied the ribbon and freed the rings.

Jack accepted hers and took her hand in his. Lily held her breath as he slipped it onto her finger.

Then it was her turn to glide the golden circle onto Jack's hand.

The priest finished with the words that joined them together and said, "You may kiss your bride."

The congregation roared their approval, hats flew into the air and Nala began to howl. But Lily did not hear it, for she was in Jack's arms, right where she belonged and she was certain that their adventures together had only just begun.

* * * * *

Harlequin Romantic Suspense presents the latest book in the scorching new KELLEY LEGACY *miniseries from best-loved veteran series author Carla Cassidy*

Scandal is the name of the game as the Kelley family fights to preserve their legacy, their hearts...and their lives.

Read on for an excerpt from the fourth title RANCHER UNDER COVER

Available October 2011 from Harlequin Romantic Suspense

"Would you like a drink?" Caitlin asked as she walked to the minibar in the corner of the room. She felt as if she needed to chug a beer or two for courage.

"No, thanks. I'm not much of a drinking man," he replied.

She raised an eyebrow and looked at him curiously as she poured herself a glass of wine. "A ranch hand who doesn't enjoy a drink? I think maybe that's a first."

He smiled easily. "There was a six-month period in my life when I drank too much. I pulled myself out of the bottom of a bottle a little over seven years ago and I've never looked back."

"That's admirable, to know you have a problem and then fix it."

Those broad shoulders of his moved up and down in an easy shrug. "I don't know how admirable it was, all I knew at the time was that I had a choice to make between living and dying and I decided living was definitely more appealing."

She wanted to ask him what had happened preceding that six-month period that had plunged him into the bottom of the bottle, but she didn't want to know too much about him. Personal information might produce a false sense of intimacy that she didn't need, didn't want in her life.

"Please, sit down," she said, and gestured him to the table. She had never felt so on edge, so awkward in her life.

"After you," he replied.

She was aware of his gaze intensely focused on her as she rounded the table and sat in the chair, and she wanted to tell him to stop looking at her as if she were a delectable dessert he intended to savor later.

Watch Caitlin and Rhett's sensual saga unfold amidst the shocking, ripped-from-the-headlines drama of the Kelley Legacy miniseries in

RANCHER UNDER COVER

Available October 2011 only from Harlequin Romantic Suspense, wherever books are sold.

HRSEXP1011

Harlequin
Presents®